PATTY'S BUTTERFLY DAYS

CAROLYN WELLS

1st WORLD
LIBRARY
Literary Society

Patty's Butterfly Days

Carolyn Wells

© 1st World Library – Literary Society, 2005
PO Box 2211
Fairfield, IA 52556
www.1stworldlibrary.org
First Edition

LCCN: 2004195588

Softcover ISBN: 1-4218-0409-3
Hardcover ISBN: 1-4218-0309-7
eBook ISBN: 1-4218-0509-X

Purchase *"Patty's Butterfly Days"*
as a traditional bound book at:
www.1stWorldLibrary.org/purchase.asp?ISBN=1-4218-0409-3

1st World Library Literary Society is a nonprofit
organization dedicated to promoting literacy by:

- Creating a free internet library accessible from any computer worldwide.
- Hosting writing competitions and offering book publishing scholarships.

Patty's Butterfly Days
contributed by Tim, Ed & Rodney
in support of
1st World Library Literary Society

CONTENTS

I. DIFFERENT OPINIONS.................................... 7

II. MONA'S PLAN.. 18

III. SUSAN TO THE RESCUE........................... 29

IV. A PERFECTLY GOOD CHAPERON............. 41

V. A DINNER PARTY 52

VI. AUNT ADELAIDE...................................... 64

VII. A GARDEN PARTY 77

VIII. THE HOUSE PARTY ARRIVES 90

IX. BIG BILL FARNSWORTH.......................... 101

X. JUST A SHORT SPIN 114

XI. THE WORST STORM EVER!..................... 127

XII. A WELCOME SHELTER 140

XIII. AT DAISY'S DICTATION 150

XIV. PAGEANT PLANS.................................... 165

XV. IN THE ARBOUR...................................... 177

XVI. THE SPIRIT OF THE SEA........................ 192

XVII. THE APPLE BLOSSOM DANCE 204

XVIII. A COQUETTISH COOK 218

XIX. A FORCED MARCH................................. 231

XX. GOOD-BYE FOR NOW 244

CHAPTER I

DIFFERENT OPINIONS

"Different men are of different opinions; some like apples, some like inions," sang Patty, as she swayed herself idly back and forth in the veranda swing; "but, truly-ooly, Nan," she went on, "I don't care a snipjack. I'm quite ready and willing to go to the White Mountains, - or the Blue or Pink or even Lavender Mountains, if you like."

"You're willing, Patty, only because you're so good-natured and unselfish; but, really, you don't want to go one bit."

"Now, Nan, I'm no poor, pale martyr, with a halo roundy-bout me noble brow. When we came down here to Spring Beach, it was understood that we were to stay here part of the summer, and then go to the mountains. And now it's the first of August and I've had my innings, so it's only fair you should have your outing."

Though Patty's air was gay and careless, and Patty's tones were sincere, she was in reality making an heroic self-sacrifice, and Nan knew it. Patty loved the seashore; she had been there three months, and loved it better every day.

But Nan cared more for the mountains, and longed to get away from the sunny glare of the sea, and enjoy the shaded walks and drives of higher altitudes. However, these two were of unselfish nature, and each wanted to please the other. But as Patty had had her wish for three months, it was certainly fair that Nan should be humoured for the rest of the summer.

The season had done wonders for Patty, physically. Because of her outdoor life, she had grown plumper and browner, her muscles had strengthened, and her rosy cheeks betokened a perfect state of health. She was still slender, and her willowy figure had gained soft curves without losing its dainty gracefulness.

And Patty was still enthusiastically devoted to her motor-car. Indeed, it was the realisation that she must leave that behind that made her so opposed to a trip to the mountains.

Mr. Fairfield and Nan had both dilated on the charms and beauties of mountain scenery, on the joys and delights of the gay mountain hotels, but though Patty listened amiably, she failed to look upon the matter as they did. At first, she had declared her unwillingness to go, and had tried to devise a way by which she might remain at Spring Beach, while her parents went to the mountains. But no plan of chaperons or visiting relatives seemed to satisfy Mr. Fairfield of its availability.

"I can't see it, Patty," he would say; "there is no chaperon for you that we know of, and I wouldn't leave you here with some stranger obtained by advertisement. Nor have we any relatives who could come to look after you. If Nan's mother could come, that would do beautifully. But Mrs. Allen is in Europe and none of your aunts could leave her own family. No, girlie, I can't see any way to separate our family."

So Patty, with her unfailing good nature, had agreed to go to the White Mountains with the others. She admitted, herself, that she'd probably have a good time, as she always did everywhere, but still her heart clung to "The Pebbles," as they called their seashore home, and she silently rebelled when she thought of "Camilla," her swift little electric runabout.

Patty drove her own car, and she never tired of spinning along the shore roads, or inland through the pine groves and laurel jungles. She had become acquainted with many young people, both cottagers and hotel guests, and the outlook for a pleasant summer and fall at Spring Beach was all that could be desired from her point of view. But before they left the city in the spring, Patty had known that Nan preferred mountain localities and had agreed to the seashore house for her sake; so, now, it was Patty's turn to give up her preference for Nan's.

And she was going to do it, - oh, yes, - she was going to do it cheerfully and even gaily. But, though she tried to pretend she didn't care, Nan knew she did care, and she had tried hard to think of some way that Patty might be left behind. Nan would willingly have given up her own desires, and stayed at Spring Beach all summer, but her husband wouldn't hear of it. Mr. Fairfield said that justice demanded a fair division of the season, and already three months had been spent at the seashore, so August and September must be spent in the mountains.

His word was law, and, too, Patty realised the fairness of the plan, and gracefully submitted to Fate. So, as the first of August was in the very near future, Patty and Nan were discussing details of the trip.

"It almost seems as if you might take your motor-car, Patty," said Nan, reflectively.

"I thought so, too, at first; but father says not. You see, not all mountain roads are modern and well-kept, and, of course, we'll be moving on, now and then, and Camilla IS a nuisance as luggage. Now, Nan, no more suggestions, or regrets, or backward glances. I'm going to the mountains, NOT like the quarry-slave at night, but like a conquering hero; and I shall have all the mountaineers at my feet, overwhelming me with their devoted attentions."

"You probably will, Patty; you're easily the most popular girl at Spring Beach, and if the 'mountaineers' have any taste in such matters -"

"There, there, Nan, don't make me blush. I'm 'popular,' as you call it, because I have such a delightful home, and such an attractive stepmother to make it pleasant for my callers! And, by the same token, here are a few of them coming now."

Two laughing girls, and a good-looking young man came in at the gate, and strolled along the drive to the veranda, where Patty and Nan sat.

Lora and Beatrice Sayre were of the "butterfly" type, and their pale-coloured muslin gowns, broad hats, and fluttering scarfs made the description appropriate. Jack Pennington was just what he looked like, a college youth on his vacation; and his earnest face seemed to betoken a determination to have the most fun possible before he went back to grind at his books.

"Hello," cried Patty, who was not given to dignified forms of salutation.

The trio responded gaily, and coming up on the veranda, selected seats on the wicker chairs, or couches, or the porch railing, as suited their fancy.

"I say," began young Pennington, conversationally, "we can't let you go away, Patty. Why, week after next we're going to have the Pageant, and there are forty-'leven other pleasant doings before that comes off."

"Yes," chimed in Lora Sayre, "we can't get along without our Pitty-Pat. DO don't go away, Sunshine!"

"But suppose I want to go," said Patty, bravely trying to treat the subject lightly; "suppose I'm just crazy to go to that stunning big hotel up in the White Mountains, and have the time of my life!"

"Suppose the moon is made of green pumpkins!" scoffed Jack. "You don't want to go at all, and you know it! And then, think of the girls, - and boys, - you leave behind you! Your departure is a national calamity. We mourn our loss!"

"We do so!" agreed Beatrice. "Why, Patty, I'm going to have a house party next week, and we'll have lots of fun going on. Can't you wait over for that?"

"No, I can't," and Patty spoke a little shortly, for these gay plans made her long more than ever to stay at

Spring Beach. "So don't let's talk any more about me. Tell me about the Pageant, - will it be fine?"

"Oh, yes," said Jack, "the biggest thing ever. Sort of like a Durbar, you know, with elephants and -"

"No, it isn't going to be like that," said Lora. "They've given up that plan. It's going to be ever so much nicer than that! They're going to have -"

"Don't tell me!" cried Patty, laughing, as she clapped her hands over her ears. "I'd rather not hear about it! I suppose you'll be queen of it, whatever it is, Lora?"

"I'll have a chance at it, if you're not here! That's the only comfort about your going away. Somebody else can be the Belle of Spring Beach for a time."

The good-natured laughter in Lora's eyes took all sting from her words, and, indeed, it was an acknowledged fact that Pretty Patty was the belle of the little seashore colony.

"I'm awfully sorry about it," began Nan, but Patty stopped her at once.

"There's nothing to be sorry about, Madame Nan," she cried, gaily; "these provincial young people don't appreciate the advantages of travel. They'd rather stay here in one place than jog about the country, seeing all sorts of grand scenery and sights! Once I'm away from this place I shall forget all about its petty frolics and its foolish parties."

"Yes, you WILL!" exclaimed Jack, not at all impressed by Patty's statements, for he knew how untrue they were.

"And the Country Club summer dance!" said Beatrice, regretfully. "Patty, how can you be reconciled to missing that? It's the event of the season! A fancy dance, you know. A sort of Kirmess. Oh, DON'T go away!"

"Don't go away!" echoed Lora, and Jack broke into one of the improvised songs for which he was famous:

"Don't go away from us, Patty, Patty,
We can't part with the likes of you!
Stay, and be Queen of the Pageant, Patty,
Patty, Patty, tender and true.
Though you are not very pretty, Patty,
Though you are liked by a very few;
We will put up with you, Patty, Patty, -
Patty, Patty, stay with us, do!"

The rollicking voice and twinkling eyes, which were Jack's chief charms, made Patty laugh outright at his song. But, not to be outdone in fun, and also, to keep herself from growing serious, she sang back at him:

"I don't want to stay at this place,
I don't like it any more!
I am going to the mountains,
Where I've never been before.
I shall tramp the mountain pathways,
I shall climb the mountain's peak;
I don't want to stay in this place,
So I'll go away next week!"

"All right for you!" declared Jack. "Go on, and joy go with you! But don't you send me any picture postcards of yourself lost in a perilous mountain fastness, - 'cause I won't come and rescue you. So there!"

"What is a mountain fastness?" demanded Patty. "It sounds frisky."

"It isn't," replied Jack; "it's a deep gorge, with ice-covered walls and no way out; and as the darkness falls, dreadful growls are heard on all sides, and wild animals prowl - and prowl - and prow-ow-owl!"

Jack's voice grew deep and terrible, as he suggested the awful situation, but Patty laughed gaily as she said:

"Well, as long as they keep on prowling, they certainly can't harm me. It all sounds rather interesting. At any rate, the ice-covered walls sound cool. You must admit Spring Beach is a hot place."

"All places are hot in hot weather," observed Beatrice, sapiently; "when there's an ocean breeze, it's lovely and cool here."

"Yes," agreed Lora, "when there IS. But there 'most generally ISN'T. To-day, I'm sure the thermometer must be about two hundred."

"That's your heated imagination," said Jack. "It's really about eighty-four in the shade."

"Let's move around into the shade, then," said Patty. "This side of the veranda is getting sunny."

So the young people went round the corner of the house to a cooler spot, and Nan expressed her intention of going down to the train to meet Mr. Fairfield.

"You people," began Patty, after Nan had left them, "mustn't talk as you do about my going away, before my stepmother. You see, we're going because she wants to go, but it isn't polite to rub it in!"

"I know it," said Beatrice, "but I forgot it. But, I say, Patty, I think it's too bad for you to be trailed off there just to please her."

"Not at all, Bee. She has stayed here three months to please me, and turn about is fair play."

"It's Fairfield play, at any rate," put in Jack. "You're a trump, Patty, to take it so sweetly. I wish you didn't have to go, though. '

"So say we all of us," declared Lora, but Patty ordered them, rather earnestly, to drop the subject and not refer to it again.

"You must write me all about the Pageant, girls," she went on.

"Can't I write too, though I'm not a girl?" asked Jack.

"No!" cried Patty, holding up her hands in pretended horror. "I couldn't receive a letter from a young man!"

"Oh, try it," said Jack, laughing. "I'll help you. You've no idea how easy it is! Have you never had a letter from a man?"

"From papa," said Patty, putting the tip of her finger in her mouth, and speaking babyishly.

"Papa, nothing! You get letters from those New York

chaps, don't you, now?"

"Who New York chaps?" asked Patty, opening her eyes wide, with an over-innocent stare.

"Oh, that Harper kid and that Farrington cub and that Hepworth old gentleman!"

"What pretty pet names you call them! Yes, I get letters from them, but they're my lifelong friends."

"That's the position I'm applying for. Don't you need one more L. L. F.?" But Patty had turned to the girls, and they were counting up what few parties were to take place before Patty went away.

"I'd have a farewell party myself," said Patty, thoughtfully, "but there's so little time now, and Nan's pretty busy. I hate to bother her with it. You see, we leave next week, - Thursday."

"And our house party comes that very day!" said Beatrice, regretfully. "And Captain Sayre is coming. He's the most stunning man! He's our second cousin, and older than we are, but he's just grand, isn't he, Lora?"

"Yes; and he'd adore Patty. Oh, girlie, DON'T go!"

"I think I'll kidnap Patty," said Jack. "The day they start, I'll waylay the party as they board the train, and carry Patty off by force."

"You'd have to get out a force of militia," laughed Patty. "My father Fairfield is of a sharp-eyed disposition. You couldn't carry off his daughter under his nose."

"Strategy!" whispered Jack, in a deep, mysterious voice. "I could manage it, somehow, I'm sure."

"Well, it wouldn't do any good. He'd just come back after me, and we'd take the next train. But, oh, girls, I do wish I could stay here! I never had such a disappointment before. I've grown to love this place; and all you people; and my dear Camilla!" Patty's blue eyes filled with real tears, as she dropped her light and bantering manner, and spoke earnestly.

"It's a shame!" declared Jack, as he noted the drops trembling on the long, curled lashes. "Come on, girls, I'm going home before I express myself too strongly."

So Jack and the Sayre girls went away, and Patty went up to her own room.

CHAPTER II

MONA'S PLAN

That night, when Patty was alone in her own room, she threw herself into a rocking chair, and rocked violently, as was her habit, when she had anything to bother her. She looked about at the pretty room, furnished with all her dear and cherished belongings.

"To go away from all this," she thought, "and be mewed up in a little bare room, with a few sticks of horrid old furniture, and nowhere to put things away decently!"

She glanced at her room wardrobes and numerous chiffoniers and dressing-tables.

"Live in a trunk, I s'pose," she went on to herself; "all my best frocks in a mess of wrinkles, all my best hats smashed to windmills! No broad ocean to look at! Nothing but mountains with trees all over their sides! Nothing to do but walk up rocky, steep paths to a spring, take a drink of water, and come stumbling down again! In the evenings, dress up, and promenade eighty thousand feet of veranda, AS ADVERTISED!"

Roused to a frenzy by her own self-pity and indignation, Patty got up and stalked about the room.

Carolyn Wells

She flung off her pretty summer frock, and slipped on a blue silk kimono. Then she sat down in front of her dressing-table to brush her hair for the night.

She drew out the pins, and great curly masses came tumbling down around her shoulders. Patty's hair was truly golden, and did not turn darker as she grew older.

She brushed away slowly, and looked at herself in the mirror. What she saw must have surprised her, for she dropped her brush in astonishment.

"Well, Patricia Fairfield!" she exclaimed to her own reflection. "You ought to be ashamed of yourself! YOU, who are supposed to be of amiable disposition, YOU whom people call 'Sunshine,' because of your good nature, YOU who have every joy and every blessing that heart can wish, you look like a sour-faced, cross-grained, disgruntled old maid! So there now! And, Miss, do you want to know what *I* think of you?" She picked up her hair brush, and shook it at the flushed, angry face in the mirror. "Well, *I* think you're a monster of selfishness! You're a dragon of ingratitude! And a griffin of cross-patchedness! Now, Miss, WILL you drop this attitude of injured innocence, and act like a civilised human being?"

Patty was a little over hard on herself. She hadn't at all exhibited such traits as she charged herself with, but she was not a girl to do things by halves. She sat, calmly looking at her own face, until the lines smoothed themselves out of her forehead, the dimples came back to her cheeks, and the laughter to her blue eyes.

"That's better!" she said, wagging her head at the

pretty, smiling face. "Now, never again, Patty Fairfield, let me see you looking mopy or peevish about anything! Mind, not about anything at all! You have enough blessings and pleasures to make up for any disappointments that may come to you. So, now that you've braced up, just STAY braced up! See?"

The scolding, though self-inflicted, did Patty good, and humming a lively tune, she busied herself with arranging some fans and frills in boxes to take away with her.

If stray thoughts of the Pageant or the Fancy Dance crept into her mind, she determinedly thrust them out, and forced her anticipations to the unknown fun and gaiety she would enjoy at the big Mountain Houses.

And when at last, ready for bed, she stood in front of her long cheval glass, the folds of her blue dressing gown trailing away from her pretty, lace-frilled night-gown, she shook her forefinger warningly at the smiling reflection.

"Now, mind you, Patricia, not a whimper out of you to-morrow! Not a shadow of a shade of disappointment on your fair young brow? Only happy smiles and pleasant words, and just MAKE yourself enjoy the prospect of those poky, gloomy, horrid old mountains!"

It will be easily seen that Patty was amenable to discipline, for next morning she went dancing downstairs, looking like amiability personified. Even Nan came to the conclusion that Patty was reconciled to the mountain trip, and had begun to see the pleasanter side of it.

Mr. Fairfield regarded his daughter approvingly. Though Patty had not been cross or glum the day before, she had been silent, and now she treated her hearers to a flood of gay and merry chatter.

Only a fleeting shadow across her face, or a sudden, pained look in her eyes when Spring Beach matters were mentioned, revealed to her watchful father the fact that Patty's gaiety was the result of brave and honest will-power. But such shadows passed as quickly as they came, and the girl's pleasant and sweet demeanour was not unappreciated by her elders.

She joined heartily in the plans for the mountain trip; discussed itineraries with her father, and costumes with Nan.

As the three sat on the veranda, thus engaged, a flying figure came through the gate like a whirlwind, and Mona Galbraith precipitated herself into the family group.

"Why, Mona, you look a little, - er, - hasty!" exclaimed Patty as, out of breath, their visitor plumped herself into a swing and twirled its tasselled ropes, while she regained her breath.

"Yes, - yes, - and well I may!" she panted. "What DO you think, Patty? Oh, Mr. Fairfield, DO say yes! Coax him to, won't you, Mrs. Fairfield! Oh, I can't tell you, - I daren't! I just KNOW you won't do it! Oh, Patty, do, - DO!"

Impetuous Mona had swayed out of the swing in her eagerness, and was now kneeling by Patty's side, stroking her hand, and gazing into her face with imploring eyes.

"Mona Galbraith," said Patty, laughing, "are you rehearsing for melodrama, or what? For, if so, you don't know your lines, and you're 'way off on your gestures, and - and, as a whole, your act is not convincing."

"Oh, don't say that, Patty!" exclaimed Mona, laughing herself. "ANYTHING but that! It must be convincing, - it must, - it MUST!"

"Is it meant for a roaring farce?" asked Mr. Fairfield, politely, "or merely high comedy?"

"I think it's a problem play," said Nan, laughing anew at the excited visitor, who had returned to the swing, and was vigorously pushing herself back and forth with her slippered toe.

"Let me help you, Mona," said Mr. Fairfield, kindly. "Is it something you have to tell us, - or ask us?"

"Yes, sir, yes! That's it!"

"Well, tell us, then. But take your time and tell us quietly. Then you won't get incoherent."

The quiet friendliness of his tones seemed to reassure the girl, and letting the swing stand still, Mona began:

"You see, Mr. Fairfield, - and Mrs. Fairfield, my father is going to Europe next week. It's on a business trip, and he only just found out that he had to go. He will take me with him if I want to go, but I don't! So I proposed a plan to him instead of that, which he thinks is fine. And, - and, I want to know what you think about it."

"We will probably approve of it, if your father does," said Nan, helpfully.

"Well - it's just this. For me to stay at home, and keep our house open, and have Patty stay there with me, instead of her going to the mountains with you."

"You and Patty stay there alone!" exclaimed Mr. Fairfield.

"No, sir; not alone. Father would ask his sister, my Aunt Adelaide, to stay with us, as chaperon. She's a lovely lady, and she'd be glad to come."

"Well, I don't know, - I don't know," said Mr. Fairfield. "I'm not sure I could go off and leave Patty with strangers."

"But I'm not a stranger," said Mona, "and Aunt Adelaide won't be, as soon as you know her. I haven't seen her myself for some years, but she's a lovely, sweet character, - everybody says so. And then, you see, we wouldn't have to close up our house, and Patty wouldn't have to leave Spring Beach, - and, oh, we could have lovely times!"

"How long will your father be gone?"

"Two months. August and September. He would rather take me with him, but he said if you all agreed to my plan, he would do so, too."

"Well, it's a surprise," said Mr. Fairfield, " and we'll

have to think it over, and talk it over. How does it strike you, Patty?"

Patty considered. It was her habit to decide quickly, but this was a case with several sides to be looked at. Yet, of course, it must be decided at once, for Mr. Galbraith must have time to make his preparations.

Patty's heart jumped with joy at the thought of staying at Spring Beach instead of going to the mountains. But - the joy was a little dampened at the idea of staying with Mona, and not at "The Pebbles."

"Why can't we both stay here?" she said at last. "Let Mona visit me here, and let her aunt chaperon us just the same."

"Oh, no," Mona said. "I know father wouldn't consent to that. You see, it's a great undertaking to close up our big place, and find homes for the servants, and look after the horses and gardens and all that, just for two months. Father was relieved at the thought of just walking off and leaving it all in charge of Aunt Adelaide. And then, we could have so much more room there, you know -" Mona paused, blushing. She did not want to imply that "Red Chimneys" was a grandly appointed mansion, while "The Pebbles" was only a pretty cottage, but that was what she meant.

"Yes, I know," said Nan, kindly helping her out. "You have such immense grounds, and luxuries of all sorts. Why, your place is a Pleasure Park of itself, with the pond and tennis court, and fountains and grottoes and all such things."

"Yes, it is a lovely summer place," said Mona,

earnestly, "and I should do everything I could to make Patty happy there. I know how much she wants to stay at Spring Beach, and it seemed such a satisfactory plan all round."

Patty was still thinking. But, by this time, she was wondering if she were really a selfish, disagreeable snob or not. For, the truth was, Patty did not entirely like Mona, though she had grown to like her much better than at first. Nor did she like Mona's home, with its ostentatiously expensive appointments, both indoors and out. And yet, it was exceedingly comfortable and luxurious, and Patty knew she could do exactly as she chose in every respect.

But, again, Patty was a favourite in Spring Beach society, and Mona was not. This might cause complications in the matter of invitations to entertainments. But Patty knew this would mostly redound to Mona's benefit. She would be asked on Patty's account to places where otherwise she would not have been invited. And Patty well knew SHE would be left out of nothing just because she was visiting Mona.

And yet, to accept her hospitality for two months meant to acknowledge her as an intimate friend, - a chosen companion. Was it quite honest to do this when, privately, Patty disapproved of many of Mona's ways and tastes? Then, it occurred to Patty that Mr. Hepworth had urged her to do what she could to help Mona, - to improve her manners, her dress, her tastes. Patty jumped at this idea, and then as suddenly paused to scrutinise her own motives, and make sure she was not pretending to herself that she did for Mona's sake what she was really doing for her own. But being quick at decisions, she saw at once that it was about evenly divided. She was willing, if she could, to help Mona in any way, and she felt that this justified her in accepting the offered hospitality of one whom she couldn't emulate.

Mr. Fairfield watched Patty's face closely, and knew pretty well what sort of a mental controversy she was holding with herself. He was not surprised when she said at last:

"Well, so far as I have a voice in this matter, I'd like to go. I think it's very kind of Mona to ask me, and I'd try not to be a troublesome visitor. You know, Father Fairfield, how much I would rather stay in Spring Beach than go to the mountains. And I suppose I could take my motor-car to Mona's with me."

"Yes, of course," Mona said. "And father says if I don't go to Europe, he'll buy me a runabout just like yours, and we can have lovely times going out together."

"Would your aunt come at once?" asked Nan, who wanted to know more about the chaperon who would have Patty in charge.

"Yes, father will send for her as soon as we decide. But you know, Mrs. Fairfield, I should keep house, as I always do, and Aunt Adelaide would only be with us in the cause of propriety."

Nan smiled at the thought of Mona's housekeeping, for "Red Chimneys" was so liberally provided with servants that Mona's duties consisted mainly in mentioning her favourite dishes to the cook.

"Are you sure you could behave yourself, Patty?"

asked her father, teasingly, "without either Nan or myself to keep you in order?"

"Oh, yes," said Patty, drawing down the corners of her mouth demurely. "In fact, as I should be on my own responsibility, I'd have to be even more careful of my manners than I am at home."

Mr. Fairfield sighed a little. "Well, Puss," he said, "I really wanted you with us on our trip, but as you'd rather stay here, and as this way seems providentially opened for you, I can only say you may accept Mona's invitation if you choose."

"Then I DO choose, you dear old Daddy!" cried Patty, making a rush for her father, and, seating herself on the arm of his chair, she patted his head, while she told him how glad she was of his consent. "For," she said, "I made up my mind not to coax. If you didn't agree readily, I was going to abide by your wishes, without a murmur."

"Oh, what a goody-girl!" said Mr. Fairfield, laughing. "Now, you see, Virtue is its own reward."

"And I'm SO glad!" Mona declared, fervently. "Oh, Patty, we'll have perfectly elegant times! I was so afraid you wouldn't WANT to come to stay with me."

"Oh, yes, I do," said Patty, "but I warn you I'm a self-willed young person, and if I insist on having my own way, what are you going to do?"

"Let you have it," said Mona, promptly. "Your way is always better than mine."

"But suppose you two quarrel," said Mr. Fairfield, "what can you do then? Patty will have nowhere to go."

"Oh, we won't quarrel," said Mona, confidently. "Patty's too sweet-tempered, -"

"And you're too amiable," supplemented Nan, who was fond of Mona in some ways, though not in others. But she, too, thought that Patty would have a good influence over the motherless girl, and she was honestly glad that Patty could stay at her beloved seashore for the rest of the summer.

So it was settled, and Mona went flying home to carry the glad news to her father, and to begin at once to arrange Patty's rooms.

CHAPTER III

SUSAN TO THE RESCUE

The day that Mr. and Mrs. Fairfield were to start on their trip to the mountains came during what is known as "a hot spell." It was one of those days when life seems almost unbearable, - when the slightest exertion seems impossible.

There was no breeze from the ocean, and the faint, languid land breeze that now and then gave an uncertain puff, was about as refreshing as a heat-wave from an opened furnace door.

At the breakfast table, Patty tried to persuade them not to go that day. "You'll faint in the train, Nan, on a day like this," she said. "Do wait until to-morrow."

"There's no prospect of its being any better to-morrow," said Mr. Fairfield, looking anxious; "and I think the sooner Nan gets away, the better. She needs cool, bracing mountain air. The seashore doesn't agree with her as it does with you, Patty."

"I know it," said Patty, who loved hot weather. "Well, perhaps you'd better go, then; but it will be just BOILING on the train."

"No more so than here," said Nan, smiling. She wore a light pongee silk travelling gown, which was the coolest garb she could think of. "But what's bothering me is that Mrs. Parsons hasn't arrived yet."

"Oh, she'll come to-day," said Patty. "Mona says she telegraphed yesterday that it was too hot to travel, but she'd surely come to-day."

Mrs. Parsons was the aunt who was to chaperon the two girls at "Red Chimneys," and Nan wanted to see the lady before she gave Patty into her charge.

"But it's going to be just as warm to-day," went on Nan. "Suppose she can't travel to-day, either?"

"Oh, she'll have to," said Patty, lightly. "If you can travel, I guess she can. Now, Nan, don't bother about her. You've enough to do to think of yourself and try to keep cool. I'm glad Louise is going with you. She's a good nurse, and you must let her take care of you."

Louise was the lady's maid who looked after the welfare of both Nan and Patty. But as Patty was going to a house where servants were more than plentiful, it had been arranged that Louise should accompany Nan.

"Don't talk as if I were an invalid, Patty. I'm sensitive to the heat, I admit, and this weather is excessive. But I'm not ill, and once I get a whiff of mountain air I'll be all right."

"I know it, Nancy; and so fly away and get it. And don't waste a thought on poor, worthless me, for I shall be as happy as a clam. I just love broiling, sizzling weather, and I'm sure my experiences at Mona's will be novel - if nothing else, - and novelty is always interesting."

"I hope you will have a good time, Patty, but it all seems so queer. To go off and leave you with that girl, and an aunt whom we have never even seen!"

"Well, I'll see her this afternoon, and if she won't give me a photograph of herself for you, I'll draw you a pen portrait of the Dragon Lady."

"I hope she will be a Dragon, for you need some one to keep you steady. You mean to do right, but you're so thoughtless and impulsive of late. I'm afraid it's growing on you, Patty.'

"And I'm afraid you're a dear old goose! The heat has gone to your head. Now, forget me and my vagaries, and devote all your time and attention to the consideration of Mrs. Frederick Fairfield."

"Ready, Nan?" called her husband from the doorway, and then there was a flurry of leave-takings, and final advices, and last words, and good-bye embraces; and then the motor-car rolled down the drive carrying the travellers away, and Patty dropped into a veranda chair to realise that she was her own mistress.

Not that her father or Nan were over strict with her; they merely exercised the kind and gentle supervision that every young girl ought to have. But sometimes, of late, Patty had chafed a little at their restrictions, and though she had no desire to do anything they would disapprove of, she enjoyed the novel sense of entire freedom of action. However, to be responsible to nobody at all seemed to make Patty feel an added responsibility of her own behaviour, so she went into the house, determined to do all she ought to do as mistress there. Though her time for such duties was short. The Fairfields had been obliged to leave on an early morning train, and Patty was not to go to Mona's until late in the afternoon. She had, therefore, several hours, and she went systematically to work, looking through each room to make sure all was in order for closing the house. She put away some books and some bits of choice bric-a-brac, and then went out to interview the cook.

"Yes, Miss Patty," said that worthy, in answer to her enquiries, "I've enough av food for yer luncheon, an' thin I'll dispose av the schraps, and lave the refrigerators clane an' empty."

"That's right, Susan," said Patty, in most housekeeperly tones; "and will you go away in time for me to lock up the house after you?"

"Yes, Miss; Mrs. Fairfield said we was all to go at five o'clock. Thin Miller will lock up, and give yersilf the keys."

Patty knew these matters had all been arranged by her parents, but it pleased her to assume an authority.

"Very well, Susan," she said. "And where are you all going?" "Jane, she's going to take another place, Miss; but I'm going to me sister's for a time. It's a rest I'm nadin'."

Patty looked kindly at the cook. She had never really talked with her before, as Nan a capable and sufficient housewife, and Patty was a little surprised to see what a fine-looking woman Susan was. She was Irish, but of the best type. A large, well-built figure, and a sensible, intelligent face. Her abundant hair was slightly grey, and her still rosy cheeks and dark blue eyes indicated her nationality. Though she spoke with a soft burr, her brogue was not very noticeable, and Patty felt irresistibly drawn to her.

"If you want anything, Susan," she said, "or if I can help you in any way, come to me at once. I shall be at 'Red Chimneys' for two months, you know."

"Thank you, Miss Patty. I'm thinkin' I'll be fair comfortable at my sister's. But if you do be goin' by in yer autymobile, wave yer hand, just. It'd please us all. You know the house, - down on the Scudder Road."

"Yes, I know, Susan. I often pass there, and I'll wave my hand at you every time."

Patty went back to her own room, and continued her preparations for her visit to Mona. Although "Red Chimneys" was but two blocks away, the packing to be done was the same as if for a more distant destination. Many of Patty's things had already been sent over, and now she was looking up some favourite books and music to take with her. Though, of course, she would have the keys of her own home, and could return for anything she might want.

Patty expected to go over to Mona's at five o'clock, but at about four Mona herself came flying over to "The Pebbles." She waved a yellow telegram, and before Patty heard what was in it, she divined that Mrs. Parsons had again postponed her arrival.

And this was the truth.

"Doctor fears sunstroke. Advises me to wait until to-morrow," the message read, and Patty and Mona looked at each other in blank dismay.

"Father doesn't know this," said Mona. "You see, he left this morning for New York. His steamer sails this afternoon. Of course, he was sure Aunt Adelaide would come to-day. What shall we do, Patty?"

"Well, of course it's too bad. But I'm not afraid to stay alone one night without your aunt. You've so many servants, I'm sure there's no danger of fire or burglars."

"Oh, it isn't that, Patty! I'm not afraid of such things. But, you see, we've no chaperon, - just us two girls there alone, - it isn't proper."

"Well," Patty laughed, "we can't help it. And if we have no callers, and go to bed early, no one will be the wiser, and surely, your aunt will come to-morrow."

"Oh, I hope she will! I'll telegraph her she MUST! But, - Patty, - you see - well, I shall have to tell you!"

"Tell me what?"

"Why, just this: I have invited a little party to welcome you this evening. Not many, - just about a dozen of the boys and girls. And how can we receive them without Aunt Adelaide there?"

"For mercy's sake, Mona! Why didn't you tell me this before?"

"I wanted it to be a surprise, - to welcome you to 'Red Chimneys.'"

"Yes, I know. Well, what CAN we do? We must do something! Shall I telephone to Mrs. Sayre to come and chaperon us?"

"She can't come. She has a house party coming to-day. The Sayre girls are coming to us to-night, but Mrs. Sayre has some older guests, and she couldn't come."

"Well, let's ask Mrs. Dennison. No, she's away, I know. How about Mrs. Lockwood?"

"She's ill; Lena told me so this morning. Oh, Patty, shall I have to send them all word not to come?"

"Looks that way to me. And I'm sorry to do that, too. How many are asked, Mona?"

"About twelve, counting you and me. I thought it would be such a nice welcome for you."

"And so it would! You're a dear to think of it. I suppose your things are all ordered?"

"Yes; a caterer will bring the supper. I don't know what it will be, - cook looked after it."

"Cook! Cook! Mona - I have an idea! No, I haven't, either! It's too crazy! Oh, DO you suppose we could? LET'S!"

"Patty, are YOU crazy? What ARE you talking about? And it's almost five o'clock. I suppose I must telephone them not to come! Well, I'll go home and do it, and you come on over as soon as you're ready. We'll spend the evening alone in my boudoir, and we'll amuse ourselves somehow."

"Wait a minute, Mona. Let me think. Yes, I do believe I'll do it! Mona, suppose I provide a chaperon. Will it be all right to have the party then?"

"Why, yes, if it's a proper kind of a lady, - of course it will."

Patty's eyes twinkled. "I don't know whether you'll think her a proper lady or not," she said, "but I do."

She rang a nearby bell, and when Jane answered, she asked her to send Susan, the cook, in.

Susan came, and stood respectfully awaiting Patty's orders.

"Susan," Patty began, "you're married, aren't you?"

"Yes, Miss Patty; me name is Hastings. Me husband is dead this four years, rist his sowl."

"Well, Susan, I want you to do something for me, and you may think it's very queer, but you'll do it, won't you?"

"Nothin's quare, Miss Patty, if you bid me do it. What is it, ma'am?"

Mona began to look a little scared, but Patty seemed now quite sure of her own mind, and she began, in a kind but firm voice:

"Susan, Miss Mona and I expected to have a party at her house to-night, but her aunt, who was to chaperon us, hasn't arrived. So I want you, Susan, to let me fix you up, and dress you in a proper gown, and then I want you to act as a lady who is visiting at 'Red Chimneys.' Can you do this?"

It was funny to see the varying expressions on Susan's face. Wonder, amusement, and docility followed each other in quick succession, and then she said:

"Is it a masqueradin', belike, you want, Miss Patty?"

"Yes; just that, Susan. Could you do it?"

"Av coorse I cud do it, if you be wantin' me to; but wud I look good enough, Miss?"

"You'd look all right, after I dressed you; but, Susan, could you talk with less, - less accent?"

"Me brogue, is it, Miss? Faith, an' I fear I can't be after conquerin' that! It's born in me."

"Patty," said Mona, 'I think your scheme is crazy, - perfectly CRAZY! But - if you really mean it, I'll tell you that I HAVE an Irish aunt, - at least, sort of Scotch-Irish, - and if we pass Susan off for her, the - the ACCENT won't matter."

"Just the thing!" cried Patty, gleefully. "I see my way clear now! It IS a crazy plan, Mona, I admit that, - but do you know of any better?"

"No; but, Patty, think a minute. Of course, the truth will leak out, and what will people say?"

"No, it won't leak out, - and, if it did, what harm? Susan is a nice, respectable woman, and as a member of my family is capable of chaperoning me in her own personality. But I choose this other game because it's more fun. I shall dress her up in, - in, - Susan, you couldn't wear a gown of Mrs. Fairfield's, could you?"

"The saints presarve us, Miss Patty, it wuddent go halfway round me!"

"No; so it wouldn't. Well, I'll find something. Oh, there's a gown in the attic that Mrs. Alien left here - she's Nan's mother, Mona, - that will be just right. It's grey satin and silver lace. Oh, Susan, you'll look GREAT!"

Mona still seemed a trifle unconvinced.

"Patty," she said, "you know I usually think what you do is all right, - but this, - well, this seems so very crazy."

"Mona, my child," said Patty, serenely, "I warned you that our ways might clash, and you said I might do exactly as I chose while at 'Red Chimneys.'"

"So I did, Patty, - and so I do. I'll go home now, and leave the rest of this performance to you. Come over soon, won't you?"

"Yes," said Patty, "I'll be there for dinner. Good-bye, Mona."

After Mona had gone, Patty turned to Susan.

"You know, Susan, this is to be a dead secret. Don't

ever tell anybody. And you must obey my orders implicitly. I'll pay you something extra for your trouble."

"Sure, it's no trouble at all, Miss Patty. I'd do anything for ye, whativer. But you must be afther tellin' me just what to do."

"Of course I will. And, first of all, Susan, you must go home, - I mean, to your sister's, - get your dinner there, and then come to 'Red Chimneys' about half-past seven and ask for me. They'll bring you right up to my room, and I'll dress you up as I think best. Then we'll take you down to the drawing-room, and all you'll have to do, Susan, is to sit there all the evening in a big easy chair. Can you knit, Susan?"

"Yes, Miss Patty."

"Well, bring a piece of knitting work, not an old grey thing, - a piece of nice, fleecy white wool work. Have you any?"

"I've not, Miss, but I'll get some white yarn from my sister, and start a shawl or a tippet."

"Yes; do that. Then you just sit there, you know, and knit and glance around the room now and then, and smile benignly. Can you smile benignly, Susan?"

Susan tried, and after one or two lessons from Patty, was pronounced proficient in that art.

"Then, Susan, if there's music, you must listen, and wag your head in appreciation, so! When we dance, you must look on with interest and again smile benignly. Not many of the young people will talk to you, except to be introduced at first, but if they do, answer them pleasantly, and use your brogue as little as possible. Do you understand, Susan?"

And as Susan possessed the quick wit and ready adaptability of her race, she did see; and as she adored her young mistress above any one on earth, she was only too willing to please her; and, too, the occasion had its charms for a good-hearted, hard-working Irishwoman.

She declared her willingness to obey Patty's orders, promised to keep it all a profound secret, and then went away to her sister's house until the appointed time.

CHAPTER IV

A PERFECTLY GOOD CHAPERON

It was nearly six o'clock when Patty reached "Red Chimneys." She carried a bandbox, and Miller, who followed her, carried a large suitcase, and various other parcels.

Mona met them at the door, and, directing that the luggage be sent to Patty's rooms, she carried her visitor off to her own boudoir.

"Patty," she began, "I can't let you carry out that ridiculous scheme! I'm going to telephone to the young people not to come."

"Haven't telephoned yet, have you?" enquired Patty, carelessly, as she flung herself into an easy-chair, and made vigorous use of a large fan.

"No; I waited to tell you. But I'm going to begin now," and Mona lifted a telephone receiver from its hook.

"Oh, I wouldn't," said Patty, smiling at her hostess. "You see, I've set my heart on having this party, and I'd hate to have you upset it."

But, Patty, consider how -"

"Consider, - cow - consider! Well, my fair lady, I have considered, and I must request you to hang up that telephone, and trust all to me."

When Patty adopted this tone, playful but decided, Mona knew she could do nothing with her. So she hung up the receiver, but she still showed a troubled expression as she looked questioningly at pretty Patty.

But that provoking young person only smiled at her, and slowly waved her big fan.

"Awfully warm, even yet, isn't it?" she said. "What time is dinner, Mona? I've a lot to do before that party of yours comes off."

"I ordered dinner early, so we'd have time to dress afterward. Come, Patty, I'll show you your rooms."

The two girls rose, and standing in front of Mona, Patty began to smooth the lines from the other's brow, with her own finger tips.

"There there," she said; "don't worry. Trust all to Smarty-Patty! She'll do the trick. And just turn up the corners of your mouth a little, so!"

Patty poked her forefingers into Mona's cheeks till she made her smile, and then Mona gave up.

"All right, Patty," she said. "I said you should have your own way, and so you shall! Get Miller to chaperon us, if you want to, - I won't say a word! Now, come on with me."

She led Patty across the hall to the suite of rooms

prepared for her. Like everything else at "Red Chimneys," it was on a far grander scale than Patty's own home.

There was a boudoir, bedroom, dressing-room, and bath, all fitted up in the prettiest, daintiest manner.

The ivory-tinted walls showed panels of rose-coloured brocade, ornate with gilded decorations in Empire style. The marquetry furniture and bisque ornaments carried out the scheme, and though elaborate, the rooms were most attractive and comfortable.

Patty herself preferred simpler furnishings, but she knew that Mona didn't, and she exclaimed with delight at the beauty of appointments.

"It's out best suite," said Mona, complacently, "and I've had it fixed up freshly for you."

"It's charming," declared Patty, "and I know I shall be very happy here, - IF I can have my own way!" She smiled as she spoke, but she was in earnest, too, for Mona was dictatorial by nature, and Patty by no means proposed to be tyrannised over.

"You shall, Patty! All the time you are here, your word shall be law in this house, both over the servants and myself."

"Oh, I can manage the servants," cried Patty, gaily. "I'm rather good at that. Now, if I can only manage you!"

"You can! I'll prove so manageable and docile, you'll scarcely know me!"

So, having flown her colours, Patty wagged her head sagaciously as Mona went away. "I think, Miss Fairfield," she observed to her reflection in a gold-garlanded mirror, "that you're in for a pleasant summer. Firmness tempered with kindness must be our plan; and I'm pretty sure you can, in that way, manage Mona without friction."

Humming snatches of song to herself, Patty continued to explore her new domain. The rose-coloured boudoir opened into a dainty bedroom done in white and gold. Everywhere white silk or lace curtains were looped back with Frenchy pink satin rosebuds, and the gilded furniture, with its embroidered satin cushions, made the room look fit for a princess. Patty laughed with glee, for she loved dainty prettiness and this was a novel change from her own simpler belongings.

From the bedroom she went on to the dressing-room and bathroom; the former replete with all known appurtenances to Milady's toilette, and the latter a bewildering vista of marble, silver, and glass.

Dinner was a gay little feast. Although Patty had dined once or twice before at "Red Chimneys," it had been with her parents at formal dinners, and they had been examples of the unrestrained elegance which Mr. Galbraith deemed the correct way of displaying his wealth.

The Fairfields had assumed that the overelaborateness was due to the festive occasion, but Patty now perceived that the same formality of service was observed with only the two girls at the table. And the menu was long and varied enough to have served a dinner party.

Of course, it all appealed to Patty's sense of humour, but as it was Mona's habit to dine under the super-vision of three or four serving-men, Patty was quite willing to accept the situation placidly. The servants, however, were no bar to their gay chatter. Except that they did not refer to the expected temporary chaperon, they discussed all the details of the evening's party.

Many of the courses of the dinner they dismissed without tasting, and so, by half-past seven, Patty was back in her own rooms, and Mrs. Hastings appeared promptly at the hour. A maid named Janet had been appointed to look after Patty personally, but she was dismissed, with instructions to return at eight, and then Patty began her transformation scene.

It was not accomplished without some few difficulties, and much giggling, but by eight o'clock, Patty and Mona surveyed a most acceptable looking chaperon, due to their own handiwork. Susan, or Mrs. Hastings, as they called her, looked the picture of a kindly, dignified matron. Her grey hair was done in a simple, becoming fashion, and ornamented with a spray of silver tinsel leaves. The grey satin gown of Mrs. Allen's, which Patty had appropriated without compunction, fitted fairly well, and a fichu of old lace, prettily draped, concealed any deficiencies. Though possessing no elegance of manner, Susan had quiet ways, and being observant by nature, she remembered the demeanour of ladies she had worked for, and carried herself so well that Patty and Mona were satisfied as to her ability to carry out their purpose.

Patty provided Mrs. Hastings with a black feather fan, and gave her a quick lesson in the art of using it. The piece of white knitting work proved satisfactory on inspection, and after a few final injunctions, Patty pronounced the "chaperon" complete.

Then she called for Janet, and hastily proceeded to make her own toilette. She chose a white silk muslin, dotted with tiny pink rosebuds, and further ornamented with fluttering ends of pale pink ribbon. The frock was cut a little low at the throat, and had short sleeves, and very cool and sweet Patty looked in it. Her gold curls were piled high on her head, and kept there by a twist of pink ribbon. She wore no jewelry, and the simple attire was very becoming to the soft, babyish curves of her neck and dimpled arms.

Mona appeared in rose-coloured chiffon, richly embroidered. The gown, though beautiful of itself, was not appropriate for such a warm night; but Mona had not Patty's sense of harmony, and had added a heavy necklace and bracelets of wrought Roman gold.

"You'll melt in all that toggery!" said Patty, bluntly, and Mona sighed as she saw Patty's diaphanous frock. Then, led by Mrs. Hastings, they went down to the drawing-room. They put Susan through a few lessons in introductions, practised calling her "Aunt Rachel," and bolstered up her failing courage by telling her how well she looked.

The first guest to arrive was Jack Pennington. Being a graceful mannered boy he acknowledged his introduction to Mrs. Hastings with just the correct blending of deference and cordiality. "Isn't it warm?" he said, and as this required no answer save, "It is, indeed," Susan acquitted herself creditably, and even refrained from saying "indade." Then the others came, and being a merry crowd of young people, they merely

Carolyn Wells

paused for a word or two with the elderly stranger, before turning away to their own interests. And, if by chance, one or two showed a tendency to linger and converse with her, Patty and Mona were at hand to take up the burden of the conversation.

After all had arrived, Patty conducted Susan to a pleasant seat near an open window, provided her with her knitting and a book, and gave her a whispered permission to doze a little if she wished to.

So far as the girls could see, not one of the guests had suspected that Mrs. Hastings was other than an aunt of Mona's, nor had they given her a second thought. To their minds a chaperon was a necessary piece of furniture, but of only a momentary interest. She must be greeted, and later, she must be bidden farewell, but no conversation with her between times was necessary.

The party was a pretty one. Usually, the Spring Beach people didn't care much to go to "Red Chimneys," for Mona was not a favourite. But Patty was, and, invited to meet her, every one accepted. And the large rooms, cooled by electric fans, and decorated with lovely flowers and softly shaded lights, looked somehow more attractive, now that Patty Fairfield's graceful figure was flitting through them.

After one of the dances, Patty drifted across the room and stood near Susan. That worthy was dutifully looking over her book, and occasionally glancing thoughtfully round the room.

"Keep it up, Susan!" whispered Patty. "You're a howling success! Everything's all right."

"Come for a stroll on the veranda, Patty," said Jack Pennington, coming up to her. "Mayn't I take her, Mrs. Hastings, if I'll be very careful of her?"

"Shure an' ye may, sir," said Susan, heartily, caught off her guard by this sudden request.

Jack Pennington stared at her, and Susan's eyes fell and her face turned red in deepest dismay lest she had disgraced her beloved Miss Patty. In a despairing effort to remedy her indiscretion she assumed a haughty tone and said, "You have my permission. Go with the young gentleman, Miss Patty." And with an air of having accomplished her duty successfully, Susan picked up her knitting.

Patty's twitching lips and flushed cheeks made quick-witted Jack Pennington suspect a joke somewhere, but he gravely offered his arm, and as they reached the broad veranda and walked toward a moonlighted corner of it, he said, "Interesting lady, that new aunt of Mona's, isn't she?"

"Very," said Patty, trying not to laugh.

"I always like that foreign accent," went on Jack; "is it, - er - French?"

"Well, no," opined Patty. "I don't think Mrs. Hastings IS French."

"Ah, German, then, perhaps. I've heard that particular accent before, but I can't just place it."

"I think it's sort of, - of Scotch, don't you?"

"Faith, an' I don't, thin! I'm afther thinkin' she's a daughter av ould Ireland, arrah."

Jack's imitation of Susan's brogue was so funny that Patty laughed outright.

"Perhaps the lady IS Irish," she said; "but she looks charming, and so well-dressed."

"That's so. She IS much better dressed than when I saw her last."

"Saw her last! What do you mean?"

"Well, of course I MAY be mistaken, but do you know, she looks like a - like a lady I saw once in the kitchen garden at 'The Pebbles.'"

"And pray what were you doing in that kitchen garden?"

"Well, I was helping Miller look after your motor one day, and I strolled around the house, back to the front veranda that way. And," - Jack's voice sank to an impressive whisper, - "there in the midst of the cabbages and eggplants, - there stood Mrs. Hastings, - I'm SURE it was she, - in a calico gown and checked apron!"

"Oh, Jack!" and Patty burst into laughter. "She IS our cook! Don't give it away, will you?"

"Never! Never! But WHAT a joke! Does no one know it?"

"No one at all but Mona and myself. You see -" And

then Patty told the whole story.

"Well, that's the best ever!" declared Jack as she finished. "Patty, you do beat all! No one else will guess, I'm sure, - and I'LL never tell. But it's most too good a joke to keep, now, isn't it?"

"But it's going to BE kept! Why, if some people knew of it, they'd drum me out of Spring Beach. And anyway, Jack, I wouldn't have done it, if Susan hadn't been such a dear respectable person herself."

"I'm sure she is, and to show I believe it, I'll take her out to supper."

"Gracious, goodness, Jack! I never thought of supper! Will she have to eat with us?"

"Of course she will! And, as I say, I'll take her out, so there'll be no danger of further discovery."

Patty giggled again. The idea of SUSAN being escorted out to the dining-room of "Red Chimneys"! And by Jack Pennington, the most aristocratic young man in their set!

"All right," she said. "But I must sit the other side of you. I want to keep my eye on her."

And so it came to pass that when supper was announced, Jack went up gallantly and offered his arm to the chaperon.

This seemed quite natural and proper to the other guests, and they paid little attention as Mrs. Hastings rose with dignity, and, with her escort, led the procession.

Susan was resolved to make up for her blunder, and she carried herself with an air of hauteur, and trailed the grey satin gown after her quite as if she were used to such.

"It is a beautiful home, is it not, Mrs. Hastings?" said Jack, by way of making conversation.

"It is, sir," returned Susan, careful of speech and accent, but unable to forget her deference. "Such airy rooms and fine, high ceilings."

Jack couldn't help admiring her aplomb, and he chatted away easily in an endeavour to put her at her ease.

"Will you sit here, Mrs. Hastings?" he said, offering her the seat at the head of the table, as became the chaperon of the party.

Susan hesitated, but catching Mona's nod of acquiescence, she sank gracefully into the armchair Jack held for her.

CHAPTER V

A DINNER PARTY

As Patty expressed it afterward, she felt as limp as a jelly-fish with the grippe when she saw Susan at the head of Mona's table! Mrs. Hastings herself seemed in no way appalled at the sparkling array of glass and silver, of lights and flowers, but she was secretly alarmed lest her ignorance of etiquette should lead her into blunders that might shame Miss Patty.

But Jack Pennington proved himself a trump. Without attracting attention, he touched or indicated which spoon or fork Mrs. Hastings should use. Or he gave her valuable advice regarding the viands.

"I say," he whispered, "you'd better duck the artichoke Hollandaise. You mightn't manage it just right. Or - well - take it, but don't attempt to eat it. You'd sure get into trouble."

Irish Susan had both quick wit and a warm heart, and she appreciated gratefully the young man's good-natured assistance, and adroitly followed his instructtions. But Jack was a daring rogue, and the temptation to have a little fun was too strong to resist.

"Are you fond of motoring, Mrs. Hastings?" he asked,

innocently, while Patty, on his other side, felt her heart beat madly and her cheeks grow red.

But Susan wasn't caught napping this time.

"Oh, I like it," she said, "but I'm not fair crazy about it, like some." She smiled benignly at Patty, and the few guests who overheard the remarks thought nothing of it.

But naughty Jack went on.

"Oh, then you know of Miss Fairfield's fad. I didn't know you knew her so well. I thought you had just arrived here. Have you been to Spring Beach before?"

Susan looked at Jack with twinkling eyes. She well knew he was saying these things to tease Patty, and she looked kindly at the embarrassed girl as she replied:

"Oh, my niece, Mona, has told me so much about her friend, Miss Fairfield, that I feel as if I had known her a long time."

Patty gasped. Surely Susan could take care of herself, after that astounding speech!

Jack chuckled silently, and as the game promised rare sport, he kept on.

"Are you fond of bridge, Mrs. Hastings?"

Susan looked at him. So far all had gone well, but she didn't know how long she could match his banter. So she favoured him with a deliberate gaze, and said, "Bridge, is it? I'm fond of the game, but I play only with expayrienced players, - so don't ask me."

"Ho! ho! Jack, that's a good one on you!" said Guy Martin, who sat within hearing. "You're right, Mrs. Hastings; he's no sort of a player, but I'm an expert. May I hope for a game with you some time?"

"We'll see about it, young sir," said Susan, with cold dignity, and then turned her attention to her plate.

In response to a desperate appeal from Patty, Jack stopped teasing, and made general conversation, which interested the young people, to the exclusion of Susan.

Then, supper over, he escorted the chaperon from the table, talking to her in low tones.

"I hope I didn't bother you," he said. "You see, I know all about it, and I think it's fine of you to help the girls out in this way."

"You helped me far more than you bothered me, sir," Susan replied with a grateful glance. "Will it soon be over now, sir?"

"Well, they'll have a few more dances, and probably they'll sing a little. They'll go home before midnight. But, I say, Mrs. Hastings, I won't let 'em trouble you. You sit in this cosy corner, and if you'll take my advice, you'll nod a bit now and then, - but don't go really to sleep. Then they'll let you alone."

Susan followed this good counsel, and holding her knitting carelessly in her lap, she sat quietly, now and then nodding, and opening her eyes with a slight start. The poor woman was really most uncomfortable, but

Patty had ordered this performance and she would have done her best had the task been twice as hard.

"You were a villain to tease poor Susan so at the table," said Patty to Jack, as they sauntered on the veranda between dances.

"She came through with flying colours," he replied, laughing at the recollection.

"Yes, but it was mean of you to fluster the poor thing."

"Don't you know why I did it?"

"To tease me, I suppose," and Patty drew down the corners of her mouth and looked like a much injured damsel.

"Yes; but, incidentally, to see that pinky colour spread all over your cheeks. It makes you look like a wild rose."

"Does it?" said Patty, lightly. "And what do I look like at other times? A tame rose?"

"No; a primrose. Very prim, sometimes."

"I have to be very prim when I'm with you," and Patty glanced saucily from beneath her long lashes; "you're so inclined to -"

"To what?"

"To friskiness. I NEVER know what you're going to do next."

"Isn't it nicer to be surprised?"

"Well, - that depends. It is if they're nice surprises."

"Oh, mine always are! I'm going to surprise you a lot of times this summer. Are you to be here, at Mona's, all the rest of the season?"

"I shall be here two months, anyway."

"That's time enough for a heap of surprises. Just you wait! But, - I say, - I suppose - oh, pshaw, I know this sounds horrid, but I've got to say it. I suppose everything you're invited to, Mona must be also?"

Patty's eyes blazed at what she considered a very rude implication.

"Not necessarily," she said, coldly. "You are quite at liberty to invite whom you choose. Of course, I shall accept no invitations that do not include Mona."

"Quite right, my child, quite right! Just what I was thinking myself."

Patty knew he was only trying to make up for his rudeness, and she looked at him severely. "You ought to be ashamed of yourself," she said.

"I am! Oh, I AM! deeply, darkly, desperately ashamed. But I've succeeded in making your cheeks turn that peculiar shade of brick-red again!"

"They aren't brick-red!"

"No? Well, a sort of crushed strawberry shading to

magenta, then!"

Patty laughed, in spite of herself, and Jack smiled back at her.

"Am I forguv?" he asked, in a wheedling voice.

"On condition that you'll be particularly nice to Mona all summer. And it's not much to your credit that I have to ASK such a thing of you!"

"You're right, Patty," and Jack looked honestly penitent. "I'm a good-for-nothing brute! A boor without any manners at all! Not a manner to my name! But if you'll smile upon me, and let me, - er - surprise you once in a while, I'll, - oh, I'll just tie myself to Mona's apron strings!"

"Mona doesn't wear aprons!"

"No, I know it," returned Jack, coolly, and they both laughed.

But Patty knew she had already gained one friend for Mona, for heretofore, Jack Pennington had ignored the girl's existence.

"What are you doing to-morrow, Patty?" asked Dorothy Dennison, as she and Guy Martin came up to the corner where Patty and Jack were sitting. It was a pleasant nook, a sort of balcony built out from the main veranda, and draped with a few clustering vines. The veranda was lighted with Japanese lanterns, whose gayer glow was looked down upon by the silvery full moon.

"We're going to the Sayres' garden party, - Mona and I," said Patty.

"Oh, good gracious!" rejoined Dorothy. "I suppose Mona will have to be asked everywhere, now you're staying with her!"

"Not to YOUR parties, Dorothy, for I'm sure neither of us would care to come!"

It was rarely that Patty spoke crossly to any one, and still more rarely that she flung out such a bitter speech as that; but she was getting tired of combating the prevalent attitude of the young people toward Mona, and though she had determined to overcome it, she began to think it meant real warfare. Dorothy looked perfectly amazed. She had never heard gentle, merry Patty speak like that before.

Guy Martin looked uncomfortable, and Jack Pennington shook with laughter.

"Them cheeks is now a deep solferino colour," he observed, and Patty's flushed face had to break into smiles.

"Forgive me, Dorothy," she said; "I didn't mean what I said, and neither did you. Let's forget it."

Glad of this easy escape from a difficult situation, Dorothy broke into a merry stream of chatter about other things, and the quartette were soon laughing gaily.

"You managed that beautifully, Patty," said Jack, as a little later, they returned to the house for the last dance.

"You showed fine tact."

"What! In speaking so rudely to Dorothy?"

"Well, in getting out of it so adroitly afterward. And she had her lesson. She won't slight Mona, I fancy. Look here, Patty. You're a brick, to stand up for that girl the way you do, and I want to tell you that I'll help you all I can."

"Oh, Jack, that's awfully good of you. Not but what I think you OUGHT to be kind and polite to her, but of course you haven't the same reason that I have. I'm her guest, and so I can't stand for any slight or unkindness to her."

"No, of course not. And there are lots of ways that I can -"

"That you can surprise Mona," interrupted Patty, laughing.

Jack smiled appreciation, and to prove it went straight to Mona and asked for the favour of the final dance. Mona was greatly elated, for handsome Jack Pennington had never asked her to dance before. She was not a good dancer, for she was heavy, physically, and self-conscious, mentally; but Jack was skilful, and guided her lightly across the shining floors.

"I'll see you to-morrow at the Sayres'," he said, as the dance ended.

"Yes," said Mona, smiling. "We're going to the garden fete. The Sayres have a house party, you know. I've always longed to have a house party."

"This would be a fine place for one," said Jack, glancing at the large and numerous rooms.

"Yes, it would. Do you suppose I COULD have one?"

"Easy as pie!" declared Jack. "Why don't you?"

"Perhaps I will, after Aunt Adelaide comes. This, - this chaperon to-night is only temporary, you know."

"Yes, I know," said Jack, but he said no more. The discovery of Susan was his secret with Patty, not with Mona. Then the young people prepared to depart, and Patty and Mona stood either side of Mrs. Hastings to assist her, if necessary, in receiving their good-nights.

Jack stood near, too, for he thought he might be of some slight help.

"Good-night, Mrs. Hastings," said Beatrice Sayre. "The girls are coming to my garden party to-morrow, and as my mother also expects guests, I'm sure she'd be glad if you would come."

Susan, much bewildered at being thus addressed, looked about her helplessly, and murmured uncertainly, "Thank you, Miss," when Jack interrupted by saying, "Such a pity, Bee, but Mrs. Hastings goes away to-morrow. Another aunt of Mona's is coming to play chaperon at 'Red Chimneys.'"

"Oh," said Beatrice, carelessly; "then this is good-bye as well as good-night, Mrs. Hastings. I've SO enjoyed meeting you."

These conventional phrases meant nothing on

Beatrice's part, but it almost convulsed Patty to hear Susan thus addressed. However, she knew she must play the game a few moments longer, and she did so, watching the thoughtless young guests as they shook hands with the masquerading COOK!

Jack Pennington was the last to go. "I say," he whispered to Patty, "it's been a great success! I don't see how you ever had the nerve to try it, but it worked all right!" Then he went away, and Patty and Mona sank limply into chairs and shook with laughter. Susan instantly returned to her role of servant, and stood before Patty, as if waiting for further orders.

"You were fine, Susan, just fine," Patty said, still giggling as she looked at the satin clad figure.

"I did me best, Miss Patty. I made some shlips, sure, but I thried that hard, ye wuddent belave! "In her earnestness, Susan lapsed into her broadest brogue, and the girls laughed afresh to see the silver headdress wag above Susan's nodding head.

"You were all right, Susan," declared Mona. "Now you can trot off home as fast as you like, or you can stay here over night, as you prefer."

But Susan wanted to go, as her duty was done, so, changing back to her own costume, she went away, gladdened by Mona's generous douceur.

"And now for bed," said Patty, and the two girls started upstairs. But after getting into a kimono, Mona came tapping at Patty's door. She found that young person in a white negligee, luxuriously curled up among the cushions of a wide window seat, gazing idly out at the black ocean.

"Patty, you're a wonder!" her hostess remarked, with conviction. "Can you ALWAYS do EVERYTHING you undertake? But I know you can. I never saw any one like you!"

"No," said Patty, complacently. "They don't catch 'em like me very often. But, I say, Mona, wasn't Susan just a peach? Though if Jack Pennington hadn't helped, I don't know how she would have behaved at the supper table."

"Isn't he a nice young man, Patty?"

"Lovely. The flower of chivalry, and the glass of form, or whatever it is. But he's a waggish youth."

"Well, he's kind. Patty, I'm going to have a house party, and he's going to help me!"

"You DON'T say! My dear Mona, you ARE blossom-ming out! But you haven't asked MY permission yet."

"Oh, I know you'll agree to anything Jack Pennington favours."

"Sure, I will! But he seems to favour you, and I don't always agree with you!"

"Well, anyway, Patty, it will be perfectly lovely, - and we'll have a gorgeous time!"

"Where do I come in? Providing cooks for chaperons?"

"Nonsense! Aunt Adelaide will come to-morrow, and

she'll do the chaperon act. Now, I'll tell you about the house party."

"Not to-night, Lady Gay. It's time for you to go beddy, and I, too, need my beauty sleep."

"You need nothing of the sort, - you're too beautiful as it is!"

"Oh, Mona, - Monissima! DON'T say those things to me! I'm but a weak-minded simpleton, and I MIGHT think you meant them, and grow conceited! Hie thee away, fair maiden, and hie pretty swiftly, too. And call me not to breakfast foods until that the sun is well toward the zenith."

"You needn't get up till you choose, Patty. You know you are mistress here."

"No, you're that. I'm merely the adviser-in-chief. And what I say goes!"

"Indeed it does! Good-night, Patty."

"Good-night, Mona. Scoot!"

CHAPTER VI

AUNT ADELAIDE

The next morning Patty was making one of her "peregrinating toilettes." She could dress as quickly as any one, if occasion required; but, if not, she loved to walk slowly about as she dressed, pausing now and then to look out of a window or into a book. So she dawdled through her pretty rooms, brushing her curly golden mop, and singing softly to herself.

"Come in," she said, in answer to a tap at her door, and Mona burst in, in a wild state of excitement.

"Aunt Adelaide has arrived!" she exclaimed.

"Well, that isn't a national calamity, is it?" returned Patty. "Why this look of dismay?"

"Wait till you see her! SHE'S a National Calamity!"

"Well, then, we must get Susan back again! But what's wrong with your noble aunt?"

"Oh, Patty, she's so queer! I haven't seen her for some years, but she's not a bit as I remembered her."

"Oh, don't take it too seriously. Perhaps we can make

her over to suit ourselves. Did you expect her so early?"

"No; but she said she came early to avoid the midday heat. It's almost eleven. Do finish dressing, Patty, and come down to see her."

"Hasten me not, my child. Aunt Adelaide will keep, and I'm not in rapid mood this morning."

"Oh, bother; come on down as you are, then. That negligee thing is all right."

"No; Aunt Adelaide might think me a careless young person. I shall get into a tidy frock, and appear before her properly."

"Well, go on and do it, then. I'll wait for you." Mona sat down to wait, and Patty dropped into a chair before her dressing-table, and soon twisted up her curls into presentable shape.

"I declare, Patty," Mona said, "the quicker you twist up that yellow mop of yours, the more it looks like a coiffure in a fashion paper."

"And, as a rule, THEY look like the dickens. But describe the visitor to me, Mona."

"No; I'll let you get an unbiased first impression. Here's Janet, now DO get dressed."

Except on occasions of haste, or elaborate toilette, Patty preferred to dress herself, but she submitted to Janet's ministrations, and in a few minutes was hooked into a fresh morning dress of blue and white mull.

"On, Stanley, on!" she cried, catching Mona's hand, and dancing out into the hall. "Where is the Calamity?"

"Hush, she'll hear you! Her rooms are just over here. She told me to bring you."

As Patty afterward confided to Mona, she felt, when introduced to Mrs. Parsons, as if she were making the acquaintance of a ghost.

The little lady was so thin, so pale, and so generally ethereal looking, that it seemed as if a strong puff of wind would blow her away.

Her face was very white, her large eyes a pale blue, and her hair that ashen tint which comes when light hair turns grey. The hand she languidly held out to Patty was transparent, and so thin and limp that it felt like a glove full of small bones. Her voice was quite in keeping with her general air of fragility. It was high, thin and piping, and she spoke as if every word were a tax on her strength.

"How do you do, my dear?" she said, with a wan little smile at Patty. "How pretty you are! I used to be pretty, too; at least, so they told me." She gave a trilling little laugh, and Patty said, heartily, "I'm sure they were right; I approve their opinion."

This pleased Mrs. Parsons mightily, and she leaned back among her chair cushions with a satisfied air.

Patty felt a distinct liking for the little lady, but she wondered how she expected to perform a chaperon's duties for two vigorous, healthy young girls, much inclined to gaieties.

"I am not ill," Mrs. Parsons said, almost, it seemed, in answer to Patty's unspoken thought. "I am not very strong, and I can't stand hot weather. But I am really well, - though of a delicate constitution."

"Perhaps the sea air will make you stronger after a time," suggested Patty.

"Oh, I hope so; I hope so. But I fear not. However, I am trying a new treatment, combined with certain medicines, which I am sure will help my failing health. They tell me I am always trying new remedies. But, you see, the advertisements recommend them so highly that I feel sure they will cure me. And, then, they usually make me worse."

The little lady said this so pathetically that Patty felt sorry for her.

"But you have a doctor's advice, don't you?" she asked.

"No; I've no faith in doctors. One never knows what they put in their old prescriptions. Now when I buy one of these advertised medicines, they send me a lot of little books or circulars telling me all about it. This last treatment of mine sends more reading matter, I think, than any of the others, and their pamphlets are SO encouraging."

"But, Aunt Adelaide," broke in Mona, "if you're somewhat of an invalid, how did you come to promise father that you'd look after us girls this summer?"

"I'm not an invalid, my dear. I'm sure a few more weeks, or perhaps less, of this cure I am trying now will make me a strong, hearty woman."

Patty looked at the weak little creature, and concluded that if any medicine could make her strong and hearty, it must indeed be a cure-all.

"May I call you Aunt Adelaide, too?" she said, gently, for she wanted to be on the pleasantest possible terms with Mrs. Parsons, and hoped to be able to help her in some way.

"Yes, yes, my dear. I seem to take to you at once. I look upon you and Mona both as my nieces and my loved charges. I had a little daughter once, but she died in infancy. Had she lived, I think she would have looked like you. You are very pretty, my dear."

"You mustn't tell me so, Aunt Adelaide," said Patty, smiling at her. "It isn't good chaperonage to make your girls vain."

"Mona is pretty, too," went on Mrs. Parsons, unheeding Patty's words. "But of a different type. She hasn't your air of refinement, - of class."

"Oh, don't discuss us before each other," laughed Mona, good-naturedly. "And I'm jealous and envious enough of Patty already, without having those traits fostered."

"Yes," went on Aunt Adelaide, reminiscently, "my little girl had blue eyes and golden hair, - they said she looked like me. She was very pretty. Her father was a plain-looking man. Good as gold, Henry was, but plain looking. Not to say homely, - but just plain."

A faraway look came in the speaker's eyes, and she rambled on and on about her lost husband and daughter, until Patty looked at Mona questioningly.

"Yes, yes, Aunt Adelaide," Mona said, speaking briskly; "but now, don't you want to change your travelling gown for something lighter? And then will you lie down for a while, or come with us down to the west veranda? It is always cool there in the morning."

"No, I don't want to lie down. I'll join you girls very shortly. I suppose you have a maid for me, Mona? I shall need one for my exclusive service."

"Oh, yes, Auntie; you may have Lisette."

"Not if she's French. I can't abide a French maid."

"Well, she is, - partly. Then I'll give you Mary. She's a good American."

"Americans have no taste. Is there a Norwegian girl on the place? I had a Norwegian maid once, and she -"

"No, there isn't," said Mona, deeming it wise to cut short another string of reminiscences. "You try Mary, and if you don't like her, we'll see what we can do."

"Well - send her to me - and we'll see."

Mona rang for Mary, and then the two girls went down to the pleasant and cool veranda.

"It's lucky you have such shoals of servants," said Patty. "At our house, we couldn't give a guest a choice of nationalities."

"Oh, Patty, isn't she a terror?"

"Who, Mary?"

"No! Aunt Adelaide! It gives me the creeps to look at her. She's so slight and fragile, I expect to see her go to pieces like a soap bubble."

"She IS like a soap bubble, isn't she! But, Mona, you mustn't talk about her like that. I feel sorry for her, she looks so ill and weak. I think we ought to do all we can to cheer her up, and to restore her health and strength. I'm sure she's refined and dainty in her way."

"Yes, she's all of that. But I don't see how she can do the chaperon act."

"Oh, well, there isn't much to do. It's only the idea of having a matronly lady here to observe the proprieties."

"But I don't believe she can do that. I think she'll take to her bed soon. She ought to go to a good sanitarium."

"Nonsense, Mona, she isn't as ill as all that! Can't you see through her? She's the sort of lady who likes to fancy she's ill, and likes to try all sorts of quack medicines."

"Well, you can look after her, Patty; you seem to understand her so well."

"All right, I will. Hush, here she comes."

Mrs. Parsons came slowly out to the veranda. She was followed by Mary, carrying a fan, a light wrap, a book, a thermometer, and a glass of lemonade.

"Sit here, won't you, Aunt Adelaide?" said Mona, politely offering a comfortable wicker chair.

"I'll try this, my dear, but I fear it's too low for me. Can you get another cushion or two?"

Mona went for more cushions, and then Aunt Adelaide had to have the chair moved, for fear of a possible draught, - though there wasn't a breath of wind stirring. Then a table must be moved nearer for the book and the lemonade, and the thermometer placed where it would get neither sun nor wind.

"I ALWAYS keep a thermometer near me," she explained, "and I always bring my own, for otherwise I can't feel sure they are accurate."

Mrs. Parsons wore a dress of light grey lawn. Though cool looking, it was unbecoming, for it had no touch of black or white to relieve its monotony, and on the colourless lady it had a very dull effect. But, though languid, Aunt Adelaide was quite able to give orders for what she wanted. She sent Mary for another book, and for more sugar for her lemonade. Then she fidgeted because a stray sunbeam came too near her.

"Mary," she said, petulantly. "Oh, I sent Mary away, didn't I? How long she's gone! Mona, can't you find a screen somewhere to shade that sun a little?"

"There are screens to roll down from the veranda roof, Aunt Adelaide; but it is so shady here, and they cut off the breeze so. However, if you want them down -"

"I certainly do," said the lady, and as Mary returned then, she lowered the rattan blinds.

But they were no sooner down than Aunt Adelaide wanted them up again, and when at last she became settled in comfort, she asked Mona to read aloud to her.

"Please excuse me," said Mona, who was thoroughly annoyed at the fussing and fidgeting ways of her aunt, "I am a very poor reader."

"I can read fairly well," said Patty, good-naturedly. "Let me try."

She picked up Mrs. Parson's book, secretly amused to find that its title was "The Higher Health," and she began to read as well as she could, and Patty really read very well.

"Don't go so fast," commanded her hearer; "valuable information like this must be read slowly, with intervals for thought." But when Patty provided pauses for thought, Aunt Adelaide said, petulantly, "Go on, do; what are you waiting for?"

At last, Patty purposely let her voice grow monotonous and low, and then, as she had hoped, Aunt Adelaide dropped into a doze.

Seeing that she was really asleep, Patty beckoned to Mona, and the two girls slipped away, leaving Mary in charge.

"Oh, Patty!" cried Mona, as soon as they were out of hearing. "Isn't it awful! How CAN we stand having such a horrid old fusser around?"

"Whoopee! Mona! moderate your language! Mrs.

Parsons isn't so very old, and she isn't horrid. If she's a fusser, that's just her way, and we must politely submit to it."

"Submit, nothing! If you think, Patty Fairfield, that I'm going to be taken care of by that worry-cat, you're greatly mistaken!"

"Stop, Mona! I won't let you call her such names; it isn't nice!"

"She isn't nice, either!"

"She's your aunt, and your guest; and you must treat her with proper respect. She isn't an old lady; I don't believe she's fifty. And she IS ill, and that makes her querulous." "Well, do you want to wait on her, and read to her, and put up with her fussiness all summer?"

"It doesn't matter whether we want to or not. We have to do it. Your father sent for her, and she's here. You can't send her away."

"I suppose that's so. But, oh, Patty, how I do dislike her! She's changed so. When I saw her some years ago, she was sweet and gentle, but not so fidgety and self-centred."

"You were so young then, Mona. You probably thought little about her character. And, too, her ill health has come, and that has undoubtedly ruffled her disposition."

"Well, she'll ruffle mine, if she stays here long."

"Of course she'll stay here, and we must make the best

of it. Perhaps we can train her to be a little less exacting. And then, too, you can arrange to have the servants wait on her. You needn't do it yourself, always."

"Patty, you're a great comfort. If anybody can train that woman, you can. So please try, for as you say, she'll have to stay, I suppose, until father comes home. Just think, she's father's own sister! But she isn't a bit like him. Dad isn't fussy at all."

"No, your father is of a lovely disposition. And so kind and indulgent to you, Mona."

"Yes; Dad is a darling. But we don't seem to get into the best society, as he expected, when he built this big house. I wonder why."

"Don't bother about that now," said Patty, who was going to talk to Mona some time on that very subject, but was not ready yet. "Now, as to Aunt Adelaide, for I may as well call her that since she wishes it. I think, Mona, the only way to manage her is to be always kind and sweet to her, but not to let her impose upon us. I can see she is rather exacting, and if we always give in to her whims, she will always expect it. So let's start out, as we mean to continue. I'll read to her occasion- nally, but I can't always be at her beck and call. Perhaps Janet can do it."

"Yes, Janet is a good reader. But, of course, Aunt Adelaide would find fault with her reading, as she did with yours."

"Yes, I expect that's her nature. But she'll be easy enough to get along with, if we all play fair. We'll have to give and take. And don't judge her by this morning. She was tired and worn, and, as yet, unused to her new surroundings. She'll feel more at home to-morrow."

"She can't ACT more at home! Well, I'll give her a trial, Patty, but I warn you, if she DOESN'T get placider, I'll suit myself with another chaperon, that's what I'll do!"

The girls did not see their visitor again until luncheon time, and then it was the same situation repeated. But few of the viands served at table were acceptable to Aunt Adelaide. She provided the butler with certain "health foods" of her own, and gave him elaborate instructions for preparing them, and then found much fault with the results of his labours. Patty had to laugh when Mrs. Parsons tasted, critically, a dish the butler anxiously offered.

"You've cooked it too much!" she exclaimed; "or, no, - you've not cooked it enough! I can scarcely tell WHICH it is, - but it isn't RIGHT!"

"I'm sorry, ma'am," said the surprised James. "Shall I cook another portion?"

"No," said Mrs. Parsons, resignedly. "I'll make out with this, though it is very distasteful."

As she had really eaten a hearty luncheon, Mona said only, "I am sorry, Aunt Adelaide; but perhaps you will enjoy the ice cream." At which she brightened perceptibly, saying:

"Yes, ice cream is my favourite dessert, and I hope, Mona, you will have it often."

After luncheon the visitor departed for her own rooms, saying, "I hope, my dears, you will excuse me now. I always take a nap at this hour, and as it is so warm I will not reappear until about dinner time."

"Very well, Aunt Adelaide," said Mona, greatly pleased at the plan. "Ring for Mary when you want her. Patty and I are going out this afternoon, so we'll all meet at dinner time."

"Yes, my dear. And will you please order iced tea sent to me at four o'clock, and have the house kept as quiet as possible during my nap hour?"

CHAPTER VII

A GARDEN PARTY

During the afternoon, an ocean breeze had the politeness to arrive on the scene, and it was pleasantly cool when the girls started for the garden party.

"Let's walk," said Patty, when Mona proposed the motor-car. "It's not far, and its lovely and cool now."

So the two girls strolled along the boardwalk, and then turned inland toward the Sayres' place.

Patty wore a white, lacy, frilly frock, with touches of pale yellow ribbon here and there. Her hat was of the broad-leafed, flapping variety, circled with a wreath of yellow flowers. Patty could wear any colour, and the dainty, cool-looking costume was very becoming.

Mona looked very well in light green chiffon, but she hadn't Patty's liking for simplicity of detail, and her heavy satin sash and profusion of jingling ornaments detracted from the airiness of her light gown. Her hat was of triangular shape, with a green cockade, and perched jauntily on her befrizzed hair, gave her a somewhat stunning effect.

"You'd look a lot better, Mona," said Patty, straight-forwardly, "if you didn't curl your hair so tightly."

"That's all very well for you to say," returned Mona, a little pettishly, "for your hair is naturally curly, and you don't have to use hot tongs."

"Some day I'll show you how to wave it more loosely; it'll be prettier than those kinky frizzes."

"Well, these won't last long. The curl comes out of my hair as soon as it's in. And it leaves straight wisps sticking out all over."

"That's just it. To-morrow I'll show you a wiser and a better plan of curling it."

"I wish you would, Patty. There are lots of things I want you to advise me about, if you will."

This showed an unusually docile spirit in Mona, and Patty began to think that she might help the girl in many ways during their stay together.

They turned in at the Sayres' beautiful home, and found the grounds gaily decked for the garden party. Bunting and banners of various nations were streaming here and there. Huge Japanese umbrellas shaded rustic settees, and gay little tents dotted the lawn.

The girls went to the veranda, where Mrs. Sayre and her two daughters were receiving their guests. There they were introduced to several out-of-town visitors who were staying with the Sayres.

Captain Sayre, in a most impressive looking white

uniform, asked Patty to walk round the grounds with him.

"For," said he, as they strolled away, "there's nothing to do at a garden party BUT walk round the grounds, is there?"

"Indeed there is!" cried Patty. "There's lots to do. There's tennis and croquet and quoits and other games I see already."

"Too hot for such things," declared the captain.

"Then, these tents all about, have interesting inhabitants. There's a fortune teller in one, I know."

"Fortune tellers are never interesting. They just make up a lot of stuff with no sense to it."

"But lots of things with no sense to them are interesting," laughed Patty. "I begin to think, Captain Sayre, that you're blase. I never met any one before who was really blase. Do tell me how it feels."

"Nonsense, child, you're poking fun at me. I'm not blase at all."

Captain Sayre was not more than five or six years older than Patty, but he had the air of a man of the world, while Patty's greatest charm was her simple, unsophisticated manner.

"I wish you were," she said, a little regretfully; "all the boys I know are nice, enthusiastic young people, like myself, and I'd like some one to be different, just for a change."

"Well, I can't. I assure you, I'm both nice and enthusiastic, if not so awfully young."

Patty smiled up at him. "Prove it," she said, gaily.

"All right, I'll prove it by poking an inquisitive nose into every tent on the place. Come on."

They went the rounds of the gay little festival, and so vivacious and entertaining did the captain prove, that Patty confessed frankly that she had misjudged him.

"You're NOT blase," she declared. "I never saw any one less so. If you fight with as much energy as you enjoy yourself you must be a fine soldier indeed!"

"Oh, I am!" returned the captain, laughing. "I'm one of Uncle Sam's noblest heroes! He hasn't realised it yet, because I've not had a real good chance to prove it, but I shall, some day."

"Perhaps you could show other people, without waiting for Uncle Sam's turn."

A slight earnestness in Patty's tone made Captain Sayre look at her quickly.

"I'll show you now," he said. "Give me chance for a brave, heroic deed, and watch me hit it off!"

"I will!" said Patty, with twinkling eyes. "But it's Secret Service. I mean Sealed Orders. I'll lead you to it, but you may 'hit it off' without realising it."

"Lead on, fair lady! From now, you are my superior officer."

But Patty turned the subject then, and the pair went gaily on, stopping often to chat with groups of young people, or to admire some decorations.

At last, Patty adroitly managed that they should pause near Mona, who stood talking with Lora Sayre and Jack Pennington. Patty's quick eyes saw that Mona was ill at ease, and that the others were including her in their conversation merely through a perfunctory politeness.

Patty, with her captain in tow, went up to the trio, and all joined in merry chatter. Then soon, with a gay, challenging glance at him, Patty said:

"Now Captain Sayre, you have the opportunity you wanted, to ask Miss Galbraith to go with you to the fortune teller's tent."

For a brief instant the young man looked dumfounded, but immediately recovering himself, he turned to Mona and said, gracefully:

"Miss Fairfield has told you of the secret hope I cherish; will you grant it, Miss Galbraith?"

Mona, flattered, and a little flustered at this attention, consented, and the two walked away together.

Jack Pennington gave Patty an understanding glance, but Lora Sayre said, "How funny for Edgar to do that!" Then realising the impolite implication, she added, "He's so infatuated with you, Patty. I'm surprised to see him leave you."

"Soldier men are very fickle," said Patty, assuming a

mock woe-begone expression; "but your cousin is a most interesting man, Lora."

"Yes, indeed; Edgar is splendid. He has lived in the Philippines and other queer places, and he tells such funny stories. He is most entertaining. But I see mother beckoning to me; I must go and see what she wants."

Lora ran away, and Jack Pennington remained with Patty.

"You're a brick!" he exclaimed; "to dispose of that marvelous military model, just so you could play with me!"

"That wasn't my only motive," said Patty, gazing after the captain and Mona - as they stood at the door of the fortune teller's tent. "He is such a charming man, I wanted to share him with my friend."

"H'm - you say that to tease me, I suppose. But I remember, before he arrived on the scene, you thought ME such a charming man that you wanted to share ME with your friend."

"Oh, yes," agreed Patty, lightly, "and you promised that you'd BE shared. So don't forget it!"

"As if I'd EVER forget anything YOU say to me! By the way, Mona says she's going to have a house party. What do you s'pose it'll be like?"

"I s'pose it'll be lovely. She hasn't talked to me about it yet, for we really haven't had time. The new chaperon came to-day."

"Is she a veritable Dragon? Won't she let you girls do anything?"

Patty laughed. "I don't think DRAGON exactly describes her. And she hasn't denied us anything as yet. But then, she only came this morning."

"I shall call soon, and make friends with her. I'm always liked by chaperons."

"Yes, Mrs. Hastings, for example," said Patty, laughing at the recollection of the night before.

"Oh, all chaperons look alike to me," said Jack. "Now, let's go over and hear the band play."

Across the garden, a fine orchestra was making music, and Patty hummed in tune, as they strolled over the lawns. As they neared a group of young people who were eagerly chatting, Guy Martin called out, "Come on, you two, you're just the ones we want."

"WHAT for?" queried Jack.

"To help plan the Pageant. You'll be in it, won't you, Patty? It's for charity, you know."

"I can't promise until I know more about it. What would I have to do?"

"Oh, you have to be part of a float. Stand on a high, wabbly pedestal, you know, and wave your arms about like a classic marble figure."

"But I never saw a classic marble figure wave her arms about," objected Patty; "indeed, the most classic ones don't have arms to wave. Look at the Milo Venus."

"I can't look at her, she isn't here. But I look at you, and I see you're just the one for 'The Spirit of the Sea.' Isn't she, Lora?"

But Lora Sayre had set her heart on that part for herself, so she said, in a half-absent way, "Yes, I think so."

"You THINK so!" put in Jack Pennington. "I KNOW so! Patty would make a perfect 'Spirit of the Sea.' I vote for her!"

"I'm not a candidate," said Patty, who had divined Lora's wish. "I won't agree to take any special part until I know more about the whole thing."

"Well, you'll soon know all about it," went on Guy. "We're going to have a meeting soon to arrange for the parts, and plan everything."

"Have that meeting at our house, won't you?" asked Patty, suddenly. "I mean at 'Red Chimneys.' Won't you all meet there?"

"Why, yes," said Guy. "We'll be very glad to. I tell you, there's lots to be done."

Patty had made her suggestion because she knew that if the committee met at "Red Chimneys," they couldn't help giving Mona a good part in the Pageant, and if not, she couldn't feel sure what might happen.

But Lora didn't look satisfied. "I thought you'd meet here," she said, "because mother is chairman of the

Float Committee."

"I know," returned Guy, "but, for that very reason, she'll have to have a lot of other meetings here. And as I'm supposed to look after the Sea Float, I thought it a kindness to your mother to have our meetings elsewhere."

"Oh, I don't care," said Lora, "have them where you like."

Lora turned to speak to some people passing, and then walked away with them.

"Now SHE'S mad!" commented Jack. "That's the beautiful part of getting up a show; all the girls get mad, one after another."

"*I'M* going to get mad!' announced Patty, deliberately.

"You are!" exclaimed Lena Lockwood, in amazement. "I didn't know you COULD get mad!"

"Patty gets about as mad as a small Angora kitten," said Jack.

"Yes," agreed Patty, "and I can tell you, kittens, like cats, get awful mad, if they want to. Now I'm going to get mad, if you people don't tell me all about this show, NOW! I don't want to wait for meetings and things."

"I'll tell you now," said Guy, speaking very fast. "It's to be a Pageant, a great and glittering Pageant, made up of floats with tableaux on 'em, and bands of music playing, and banners streaming, and coloured fire firing, all over Spring Beach."

"That tells some, but not all," said Patty. "You tell me more, Lena."

"Well, the Floats will represent the Sea and different rivers and all sorts of things like that. And they are all under different committees, and every chairman has to look after her own people."

"And whose people are we?" demanded Patty.

"Mrs. Sayre has the general committee of floats under her charge."

"But the Sea Float is my especial care, Patty," broke in Guy Martin, "and I want you to promise to be Spirit of the Sea. Won't you?"

"Not to-day, thank you. I have to think these matters over slowly. What do you want Mona Galbraith to be?"

A silence was the response to this question, and then Guy said:

"I hadn't put her name down yet, but I daresay she'll be asked to take some part."

"I daresay she WILL," returned Patty, "and a GOOD part, too! Why can't she be Spirit of the Sea?"

"Nonsense, that part requires a sylph-like girl, such as - such as you or Lora. Mona Galbraith is too heavy for any self-respecting spirit."

"Well, never mind," said Patty, "there must be plenty of other good parts that require more substantial specimens of humanity. Arrange your meetings at our house, Guy, and we'll fix it all up then."

They changed the subject then, for Mona and Captain Sayre came walking toward them.

"Get good fortunes?" asked Jack.

"Very much so," returned the captain. "Miss Galbraith is to become a Duchess later on, and I am to achieve the rank of a Rear-Admiral. What more could we ask?"

"Nothing!" exclaimed Patty. "You'll make a gorgeous Duchess, Mona. I can see you now, prancing around with a jewelled coronet on your noble brow."

"Can't you see me," said Captain Sayre, "prancing around in Admiral's regalia?"

"But I've never seen you prance at all. I supposed you were too dignified."

"You did! Well, you never were more mistaken in your life. Watch me, now." The orchestra was playing in lively time, and Captain Sayre began to do a lively dance, which was something between a Sailor's Hornpipe and a Double Shuffle.

He danced wonderfully well, and as Patty looked at him the spirit of the music inspired her, and throwing off her hat, she prettily caught up the sides of her frilled skirt, and danced, facing him. He smiled at her, changed his step to a more graceful fancy dance, and they danced an impromptu duet.

Others gathered about to watch the pretty sight, and Patty soon discovered that, though she was an accomplished dancer, the captain was far more familiar with the latest styles and steps. But he suited his mood to hers, and they advanced, retreated, and bowed, almost as if they had practised together for the purpose. Loud applause greeted them as the band ceased playing, and they were urged to repeat the dance.

"No," said Captain Sayre, laughing; "you forget it is a summer's day, and that sort of prancing is better suited to a winter evening. I'm going to take Miss Fairfield away to the lemonade tent, before she faints from utter exhaustion."

"I'm not tired," protested Patty, but her cheeks were pink from the exercise, and she went gladly for the refreshing lemonade.

"You're a wonderful dancer," said Captain Sayre. "Who taught you?"

Patty mentioned the name of the teacher she had had in New York. "But," she said, "I haven't had any lessons of late, and I don't know the new fancy dances."

"Some of them are beautiful; you really ought to know them. Mayn't I call on you, and teach you a few new steps?"

"I'd love to have you do so. I'm staying with Miss Galbraith, you know. But you're not here for long, are you?"

"I'll be here about a week, and I may return later for a

short time. At any rate we can have a few dances. I never saw any one so quick to catch the spirit of the music. You love dancing, don't you?"

"Yes, I do. But I love it more in cooler weather."

"Oh, this hot spell won't last long. And it's so cool mornings. Suppose I run over to see you to-morrow morning. May I?"

"Do," said Patty, cordially. "Mona and I will be glad to have you."

"But I'm coming to see YOU" said the captain, a little pointedly.

"You're coming to see us both," said Patty, very decidedly.

CHAPTER VIII

THE HOUSE PARTY ARRIVES

"Red Chimneys" was in a turmoil. The house party had been invited, and the house party had accepted their invitations, and all would have been well had it not been for Aunt Adelaide. Somehow or other she managed to upset every plan, throw cold water on every pleasure, and acted as a general wet blanket on all the doings of Patty and Mona.

She was not an over strict chaperon; indeed, she was more than ready to let the girls do whatever they chose; but she dictated the way it should be done and continually put forth not only suggestions but commands directly opposed to the wishes of the young people.

Often these dictates concerned the merest details. If the girls had a merry luncheon party invited, that was the very day Aunt Adelaide chose for a special rest-cure treatment, and demanded that the whole house be kept quiet as a church. On the other hand, if the girls were going off for the day, that was the occasion Aunt Adelaide felt lonesome, and declared herself cruelly neglected to be left at home alone.

But it was Mona's nature to submit to the inevitable, -

Carolyn Wells

though not always gracefully. And it was Patty's nature to smooth away rough places by her never-failing tact and good nature. The greatest trouble was with the servants. Those who came in contact with the nervous, fussy lady were harassed beyond endurance by her querulous and contradictory orders. The cook declared herself unable to prepare Mrs. Parson's "messes" acceptably, and threatened every other day to leave. But Patty's coaxing persuasions, and Mona's promise of increased wages induced her to remain.

Remonstrance with Aunt Adelaide did no good at all. She assumed an air of injured innocence, asserted her entire indifference to the details of Mona's house-keeping, - and then, proceeded to interfere just the same.

As far as possible, the girls had arranged the house party without consulting her; but, even so, she continually offered her advice and obtruded her opinions until Mona lost patience.

"Aunt Adelaide," she said, when Mrs. Parsons insisted that Patty should give up the suite of rooms she occupied to some of the arriving guests, "when Patty came to me I gave her the best rooms, and she's going to stay in them. I know Mrs. Kenerley is bringing her baby and nurse, and that's why I gave her rooms on the third floor, that the baby might not disturb any one."

"It's too high up for the dear child," argued Aunt Adelaide. "I'd like to have her nearer me."

"You wouldn't, if she's in the habit of crying all night," said Patty. "I'm quite willing to give up my pretty rooms, but Mona won't let me, and I never quarrel with my hostess' decisions."

"Meaning, I suppose, that I do," said Aunt Adelaide, querulously. "Of course, you girls know more than I do. I'm only a poor, old, set aside nobody. I couldn't expect to be listened to, even when I advise you for your own good."

Patty well knew that any response to this sort of talk was useless, so she said, lightly, "We want you mostly for ornament, Aunt Adelaide. If you'll put on one of your prettiest dresses, and some of that lovely old lace of yours, and your amethyst jewellery, and be on hand to welcome our guests this afternoon, Mona and I will relieve you of all bother about household arrangements."

This mollified Mrs. Parsons somewhat, for she dearly loved to "dress up" and receive company, so she went away to select her costume.

Patty had been at "Red Chimneys" little more than a week, but already the influence of her taste could be seen in the household. Some of the more gaudy and heavy ornaments, which had been provided by a professional decorator, had been removed, and their places filled by palms, or large plain bowls of fresh flowers.

The cook's extravagant ideas were curbed, and the meals were now less heavily elaborate, and the viands more delicate and carefully chosen. The service was simpler, and the whole household had lost much of its atmosphere of vulgar ostentation. Mona, too, was improved. Her frocks were more dainty and becoming, and Patty had persuaded her to wear less jewellery and ornamentation. Patty had also taught her to wave her hair in pretty, loose curls that were far more effective than the tight frizzes she had worn. The plans for the house party were complete, and, to the girls, entirely satisfactory.

Adele Kenerley had been a school friend of Mona's, and was coming with her husband and baby girl. Daisy Dow, another of Mona's schoolmates, was coming from Chicago, and Roger Farrington and two other young men would complete the party, which had been invited for a week.

Patty had not accomplished all her wishes, without some difficulties. Several times Mona had balked at Patty's decrees, and had insisted on following her own inclinations. But by tactful persuasion Patty had usually won out, and in all important matters had carried the day. It was, therefore, with honest pride and satisfaction that she looked over the house just before the arrival of the guests.

She had herself superintended the arrangement of the beautiful flowers for which the Galbraiths' garden was famous, and she had, in a moment of victory, persuaded Mona to put the men servants into white duck instead of their ornate, gilt-braided livery, and the maids into white linen uniforms.

"In this weather," she said, "let's make our keynote 'coolness,' and your guests will have a better time than if we overpower them with your winter splendour."

Mona began to see that coolness and splendour were rarely compatible, but she was also beginning to see things as Patty saw them, so she agreed. The girls had not dared to advise Aunt Adelaide as to costume, for just so sure as they advised something, that contradictory lady would be sure to insist on something else.

"But I think I'd better coax her to wear that purple satin," said Mona, "for if I don't, she'll surely put it on, and if I do, she won't!"

"Wait and see," said Patty. "I took pains to hang her lavender crepe de chine right in the front of her wardrobe, and I hope she'll let her eagle eye light on that, and seek no further!"

"Patty, you're a born conspirator. I hope you'll marry a foreign diplomat, and help him manage his international intrigues."

"Oh, I could manage the intrigues and the diplomat both, I expect."

"I'm sure you could! Now, let's fly and get dressed. The Kenerleys will come soon and I'm crazy to see Adele's darling baby."

Soon after, the girls going downstairs in their fresh, light summer frocks, were much pleased to see that Patty's ruse had succeeded. Aunt Adelaide was gracefully posed in a veranda chair, wearing the lavender gown, a collar of fine old lace, and her amethyst necklace. She looked gentle and charming, and seemed in high good humour.

"I hope you like this gown," she said. "I hesitated a long time, but finally chose it because it matched my necklace."

"It's lovely," said Patty, enthusiastically; "and it suits you awfully well. Look, Mona, there they come!"

Another moment, and a rosy-cheeked young matron flew into Mona's arms and greeted her after the most approved manner of reunited school friends.

"You dearest old thing!" she cried. "You haven't changed a bit, except to grow better looking! And, Mona, here's my husband, - Jim, his name is, - but HERE'S the baby!"

A nurse stepped forward, bringing a mite of humanity, who was laughing and waving her little fat arms, as if delighted to be of the party.

"What an angel of a baby!" cried Mona, taking the smiling infant in her arms. "And a solid angel too," she added, as the child proved more substantial than she had appeared.

"Yes; she's nearly two years old, and she weighs exactly right, according to the best schedules. She's a perfect schedule baby in every way."

Then the small piece of perfection was handed over to what was probably a schedule nurse, and general introductions followed.

Patty liked the Kenerleys at once. They were breezy and pleasant mannered, and had an affable way of making themselves at home.

"Mona," said Mr. Kenerley, - "I shall have to call you that, for I doubt if my wife has ever even mentioned your last name to me, and if she has, I have forgotten it, - Mona, how long does one have to be a guest at 'Red Chimneys' before he is allowed to go for a dip in that tempting looking ocean I perceive hard by?"

"Oh, only about ten minutes," said Mona, laughing at his impatience. "Do you want to go now, alone, or will you wait until later? Some men are coming soon who would probably join you for a swim. I expect Bill Farnsworth."

"DO you! Dear old Bill! I haven't seen him for years. But he's so big, he'd take up all the surf, - I think I'll go on by myself. And I know you girls have lots of gossip to talk over - so, I'll see you later."

Jim Kenerley set off for the Galbraith bathing pavilion, easily discernible by its ornate red chimneys, and Mona turned to have a good old-fashioned chat with Adele.

"Why, where is she?" she exclaimed, and Aunt Adelaide petulantly explained that Patty and Adele had gone to look after the baby. "Pretty poor manners, I call it, to leave me here all alone. It never occurred to them that I'd like to see the baby, too!"

"Never mind, Aunt Adelaide, you'll have lots of time to see that baby. And, of course, Adele wants to go to her rooms and get things arranged. You and I will wait here for the next arrivals. Laurence Cromer is due about now. He's an artist, you know, and he'll think you're a picture in that exquisite gown." Much mollified at these remarks, Aunt Adelaide rearranged her draperies, called for another cushion, had a screen lowered, and sat slowly waving a small fan, in expectance of the artist's admiration. And perhaps the artist might have given an admiring glance to the picturesque lady in lavender had it not happened that just as he came up the veranda steps Patty appeared in the doorway. Her pink cheeks were a little flushed from a romp with the baby, a few stray curls had been pulled from their ribbon by baby's chubby hands, and the laughing face was so fair and winsome that Laurence Cromer stocd stock-still and gazed at her. Then Mona intercepted his vision, but after the necessary introductions and greetings, the young artist's eyes kept wandering toward Patty, as if drawn by a magnet.

Young Cromer was a clever artist, though not, as yet, exceedingly renowned. He advertised his calling, however, in his costume and appearance. He wore white flannels, but he affected a low rolling collar and a soft silk tie. His hair was just a trifle longer than convention called for, and his well-cut features were marred by a drooping, faraway expression which, he fondly hoped, denoted soulfulness.

Patty laughed gaily at him.

"Don't stare at me, Mr. Cromer," she said, saucily. "Baby May pulled my hair down, but I have the grace to be ashamed of my untidiness."

"It's exquisite," said Cromer, looking at her admiringly; "a sweet disorder in the dress."

"Oh, I know that lady you quote! She always had her shoestrings untied and her hat on crooked!"

Cromer looked amazed, as if a saint had been guilty of heresy, and Patty laughed afresh at his astonished look.

"If you want to see sweet disorder in dress, here's your chance," cried Mona. "Here comes Daisy Dow, and she's one who never has her hat on straight, by any chance!"

Sure enough, as a big car whizzed up under the porte-cochere, a girl jumped out, with veils flying, coat flapping, and gloves, bag, and handkerchief dropping, as she ran up the steps.

"Here I am, Mona!" she cried, and her words were unmistakably true.

Daisy Dow was from Chicago, and she looked as if she had blown all the way from there to Spring Beach. She was, or had been, prettily dressed, but, as Mona had predicted, her hat was awry, her collar askew, and her shoelace untied.

The poetical idea of "a sweet disorder in the dress" was a bit overdone in Daisy's case, but her merry, breezy laugh, and her whole-souled joy at seeing Mona again rather corresponded with her disarranged finery.

"I'm all coming to pieces," she said, apologetically, as she was introduced to the others. "But we flew along so fast, it's a wonder there's anything left of me. Can't I go and tidy up, Mona?"

"Yes, indeed. Come along with me, Daisy. They're all here now, Patty, except Bill and Roger. You can look after them."

"All right, I will. I don't know Mr. Bill, but that won't matter. I know Roger, and of course the other one will be the gentle Bill."

"'Gentle' is good!" laughed Mona. "Little Billy is about six feet eight and weighs a ton."

"That doesn't frighten me," declared Patty, calmly. "I've seen bigger men than that, if it was in a circus! Skip along, girls, but come back soon. I think this house party is too much given to staying in the house. Are you for a dip in the ocean before dinner, Mr. Cromer?"

"No; not if I may sit here with you instead."

"Oh, Aunt Adelaide and I are delighted to keep you here. All the guests seem to run away from me. I know not why!"

Naughty Patty drew a mournful sigh, and looked as if she had lost her last friend, which look, on her pretty, saucy face, was very fetching indeed.

"I'll never run away from you!" declared Mr. Cromer, in so earnest a tone that Patty laughed.

"You'd better!" she warned. "I'm so contrary minded by nature that the more people run away from me the better I like them."

"Ah," said Laurence Cromer, gravely; "then I shall start at once. Mrs. Parsons, will you not go for a stroll with me round the gardens?"

Aunt Adelaide rose with alacrity, and willingly started off with the young artist, who gave not another glance in Patty's direction.

"H'm," said Patty to herself, as the pair walked away.

"H'm! I rather like that young man! He has some go to him." She laughed aloud at her own involuntary joke, and stood, watching Aunt Adelaide's mincing steps, as she tripped along the garden path.

As Patty stood thus, she did not see or hear a large and stalwart young man come up on the veranda, and, smiling roguishly, steal up behind her. But in a moment, she felt herself clasped in two strong arms, and a hearty kiss resounded on her pink cheek.

CHAPTER IX

BIG BILL FARNSWORTH

"How are you?" exclaimed a voice as hearty as the kiss, and Patty, with a wild spring, jumped from the encircling arms, and turned to face a towering giant, who, she knew at once, must be Mr. Farnsworth.

"How DARE you!" she cried, stamping her foot, and flashing furious glances, while her dimpled cheeks burned scarlet.

"Whoopee! Wowly-wow-wow! I thought you were Mona! Oh, can you EVER forgive me? But, no, of course you can't! So pronounce my doom! Shall I dash myself into the roaring billows and seek a watery grave? Oh, no, no! I see by your haughty glare that is all too mild a punishment! Then, have me tarred and feathered, and drawn and quartered and ridden on a rail! Send for the torturers! Send for the Inquisitioners! But, remember this! I didn't know I was kissing a stranger. I thought I was kissing my cousin Mona. If I had known, - oh, my dear lady, - if I had KNOWN, - I should have kissed you TWICE!"

This astonishing announcement was doubtless induced by the fact that Patty had been unable to resist his wheedlesome voice and frank, ingenuous manner, and she had indulged in one of her most dimpled smiles.

With her face still flushed by the unexpected caress, and her golden curls still rumpled from the baby's mischievous little fingers, Patty looked like a harum-scarum schoolgirl.

"Be careful," she warned, shaking a finger at him. "I was just about to forgive you because of your mistake in identity, but if you make me really angry, I'll NEVER forgive you."

"Come back, and ALL will be forgiven," said the young man, mock-dramatically, as he held out his arms for a repetition of the scene.

"This is your punishment," said Patty, gaily, paying no attention to his fooling. "You are not to tell of this episode! I know you'll want to, for it IS a good joke, but I should be unmercifully teased. And as you owe me something for - for putting me in a false position -"

"Delightful position!" murmured the young man.

"You owe me SOMETHING," went on Patty, severely, "and I claim your promise not to tell any one, - not even Mona, - what you did."

"I WON'T tell," was the fervent reply. "I swear I won't tell! It shall be OUR secret, - yours and mine. Our sweet secret, and we'll have another some day."

"What!"

"Another secret, I mean. What DID you think I meant? Any one is liable to have a secret, - any two, I mean.

And we might chance to be the two."

"You're too big to talk such nonsense," and Patty ran a scornful eye over the six feet three of broad and weighty masculinity.

"Oh, I KNOW how big I am. PLEASE don't rub THAT in! I've heard it ever since I was out of dresses. Can't you flatter me by pretending I'm small?"

"I could make you FEEL small, if I told you what I really thought of you."

"Well, do that, then. What DO you think of me?"

"I think you very rude and -"

"You don't think any such thing, - because you KNOW I mistook you for Mona, and it's not rude to kiss one's cousin."

"Is she your cousin? She never told me so."

"Well, her grandfather's stepdaughter's sister-in-law married my grandmother's second cousin twice removed."

"Oh, then you're not very nearly related."

"No; that's why we don't look more alike. But, do you know my name? Or shall I introduce myself?"

"I fancy you're Big Bill Farnsworth, aren't you?"

"Yes, - but DON'T call me big, PLEASE!"

"No, I'll call you Little Billee. How's that?"

"That's lovely! Now, what may I call you?"

"Miss Fairfield."

The big man made an easy and graceful bow. "I am delighted to meet you, Miss Fair - Fair, with golden hair. Pardon me, I've a terrible memory for names, but a good reserve fund of poetry."

"Miss Fairfield, my name is. Pray don't forget it again."

"If you're so curt, I shall think it's a Fairfield and no favour! You're not mad at me, are you?"

"Certainly not. One can't get mad at an utter stranger."

"Oh, I don't think people who kiss people can be classed as utter strangers."

"Well, you will be, if you refer to that mistake again! Now, remember, I forbid you ever to mention it, - to me, or to any one else. Here comes Mona."

Mona and Daisy Dow appeared in the doorway, and seeing Bill, made a dash at him. The young man kissed Mona heartily, and as he did so, he smiled at Patty over Mona's shoulder. He shook hands with Daisy, and soon the three were chatting gaily of old school days.

Then Roger Farrington came. Not all of Patty's New York friends had liked Mona, but Roger had always declared the girl was a fine nature, spoiled by opulent surroundings. He had gladly accepted the invitation to the house party, and came in anticipation of an all-round good time.

"Hooray! Patty! Here's me!" was his salutation, as he ran up the steps.

"Oh, Roger!" cried Patty, and she grasped his hand and showed unfeigned gladness at seeing him. Patty was devoted to her friends, and Roger was one of her schoolday chums. Mona came forward and greeted the new guest, and introduced him to the strangers.

"Isn't this just too downright jolly!" Roger exclaimed, as he looked at the sea and shore, and then brought his gaze back to the merry group on the veranda. "Haven't you any chaperon person? Or are we all kids together?"

"We have two chaperons," announced Patty, proudly. "One, you may see, just down that rose path. The lady in trailing lavender is our house chaperon, Mrs. Parsons. The impressive looking personage beside her is an artist of high degree. But our other chaperon, - ah, here she comes! Mrs. Kenerley."

Adele Kenerley appeared then, looking very sweet and dainty in her fresh summer frock, and laughingly expressed her willingness to keep the house party in order and decorum.

"It won't be so very easy, Mrs. Kenerley," said Roger. "My word for it, these are wilful and prankish girls. I've known Miss Fairfield for years, and she's capable of any mischief. Miss Galbraith, now, is more sedate."

"Nonsense!" cried Patty. "I'm the sedate one."

"You don't look it," observed Mona. "Your hair is a sight!"

"It is," said Laurence Cromer, coming up and catching the last remark; "a sight for gods and men! Miss Fairfield, I beseech you, don't do it up in fillets and things; leave it just as it is, DO!"

"Indeed I won't," said Patty, and she ran away to her own room to put her curly locks in order. She was quite shocked at the mirrored picture of tousled tresses, and did it all up a little more severely than usual, by way of amends.

"May I come in?" and Daisy Dow, after a quick tap at the door, walked in, without waiting for an answer.

"What lovely hair!" she exclaimed, as Patty pushed in more and more hairpins. "You're a perfect duck, anyway. I foresee I shall be terribly jealous of you. But I say, Patty, - I MAY call you Patty, mayn't I? - don't you dare to steal Big Bill Farnsworth away from me! He's my own particular property and I don't allow trespassing."

There was an earnest tone underlying Daisy's gay words that made Patty look up at her quickly. "Are you engaged to him?" she asked.

"No, - not exactly. At least, it isn't announced. But -"

"Oh, pshaw, don't trouble to explain. I won't bother your big adorer. But if he chooses to speak to me, I shan't be purposely rude to him. I like boys and young men, Miss Dow, and I like to talk and play and dance with them. But I've no SPECIAL interest in any ONE, and if you have, I shall certainly respect it, - be sure of that."

"You're a brick, Patty! I was sure you were the minute I laid my two honest grey eyes on you. But you're 'most too pretty for my peace of mind. Bill adores pretty girls."

"Oh, don't cross bridges before you come to them. Probably he'll never look at little me, and if he should, I'll be too busy to see him. There ARE others, you know."

Reassured by Patty's indifference, Daisy vowed her everlasting friendship and adoration, and the two went downstairs arm in arm.

The veranda presented a gay scene - afternoon tea was in progress, and as some of the Spring Beach young people had dropped in, there were several groups at small tables, or sitting on the veranda steps and railings.

"I've saved a lovely seat for you," said Laurence Cromer, advancing to Patty; "just to show you that I'm of a forgiving nature."

"Why, what have I done to be forgiven for?" asked Patty, opening her blue eyes wide in surprise.

"You've spoiled your good looks, for one thing. You HAD a little head sunning over with curls, and now you have the effect of a nice little girl who has washed her face and hands and neatly brushed her hair."

"But one can't go around like Slovenly Peter," said

Patty, laughing, as she took the wicker chair he placed for her.

"Why not, if one is a Pretty Peter?"

"Oh, pshaw, I see you don't know me very well. I never talk to people who talk about me."

"Good gracious, how can they help it?" "Well, you see, I'm accustomed to my girl and boy friends, whom I've known for years. But here, somehow, everybody seems more grown up and societyfied."

"How old are you?"

"It's my impression that that's a rude question, though I'm not sure."

"It isn't, because you're not old enough to make it rude. Come, how old?"

"Nineteen, please, sir."

"Well, that's quite old enough to drop boy and girl ways and behave as a grown-up."

"But I don't want to," and Patty's adorable pout proved her words.

"That doesn't matter. Your 'reluctant feet' have to move on whether they wish to or not. Are you bashful?"

"Sorta," and Patty put her finger in her mouth, with a shy simper.

"You're anything but bashful! You're a coquette!"

"Oh, no!" and Patty opened her eyes wide in horror. "Oh, kind sir, DON'T say THAT!"

But Cromer paid no heed to her words; he was studying her face. "I'm going to paint you," he announced, "and I shall call it 'Reluctant Feet.' Your head, with its aureole of curls; your wide eyes, your baby chin -"

"Oh, Roger!" cried Patty, as young Farrington came toward her. "What DO you think? Mr. Cromer is going to paint a picture of my head and call it 'Reluctant Feet'! He says so."

"Yes," said Cromer, unconscious of any absurdity; "Miss Fairfield is a fine subject."

"That's better than being called an object," said Roger, joining them, "and you DID look an object, Patty, when I arrived! Your wig was all awry, - and -"

"You haven't a soul for art?" said Cromer, looking solemnly at Roger.

"No, I haven't an artful soul, I fear. How are you getting along, Patty, down here without your fond but strict parents?"

"Getting along finely, Roger. Aunt Adelaide plays propriety, and Mona and I keep house."

"H'm, I'm 'fraid I scared off our long-haired friend," said Roger, as Cromer rose and drifted away. "Never mind, I want to talk to you a little myself. I say, Patsy, don't you let these men flatter you till you're all puffed up with pride and vanity."

"Now, Roger, AM I that kind of a goose?"

"Well, you're blossoming out so, and getting so growny-uppy looking, I'm 'fraid you won't be my little Patty-friend much longer."

"'Deed I shall! Don't you worry about that. How do you think Mona is looking?"

"Fine! Lots better than when I saw her in May. She dresses better, don't you think?"

"Yes, I guess she does," said Patty, demurely, with no hint as to WHY Mona's appearance had improved. "She's an awfully nice girl, Roger."

"Yes, I always said so. And you and she help each other. Sort of reaction, you know. What do we do down here?"

"Oh, there are oceans of things planned. Parties of all sorts, and picnics, and dances, and motor trips, and every old thing. How long can you stay?"

"I'm invited for a week, but I may have to go home sooner. Isn't that Western chap immense?"

For some ridiculous reason, Patty blushed scarlet at the mere mention of Mr. Farnsworth.

"What the - oh, I say, Patty! You're not favouring him, are you? Why, you've only just met him to-day, haven't you?"

"Yes, certainly; I never saw him before. No, I'm not favouring him, as you call it."

"Then why are you the colour of a hard-boiled lobster? Patty! Quit blushing, or you'll burn up!"

"Don't, Roger; don't be silly. I'm NOT blushing."

"Oh, no! You're only a delicate shade of crimson vermilion! Well, if you want him, Patty, I'll get him for you. Do you want him now?"

"No! of course I don't! Do be still, Roger! And stop that foolish smiling! Well, then, I'm going to talk to Adele Kenerley."

Patty ran away from Roger, who was decidedly in a teasing mood, and seated herself beside the pretty young matron.

"Such a GOOD child," Mrs. Kenerley was saying; "she NEVER cries, and she's SO loving and affectionate."

"Oh, she's a heavenly baby!" cried Mona, in raptures of appreciation, and then along came the baby's father, fresh from his ocean dip.

"You must choke off my wife," he said, smiling, "if she gets started on a monologue about that infant prodigy! She can keep it up most of the hours out of the twenty-four, and go right over it all again next day!"

"And why not?" cried Mona. "SUCH a baby deserves appreciation. I can hardly wait till to-morrow to wake her up and play with her."

"She's a good enough kiddy," said the proud young father, trying to hide his own enthusiasm.

"Now, Jim," cried his wife, "you know perfectly well you're a bigger idiot about that child than I am! Why, would you believe, Mona -"

"There, there, Adele, if you're going to tell anecdotes of my parental devotion, I'm going to run away! Come on, Farnsworth, let's go for a stroll, and talk over old times."

The two men walked off together, and the party generally broke up. Most of them went to their rooms to rest or dress for dinner, and Patty concluded that she would grasp the opportunity to write a letter to Nan, a task which she enjoyed, but rarely found time for.

"The house party is upon us," she wrote, "and, though they're really very nice, they ARE a little of the west, westy. But there's only one girl, Daisy Dow, who's MUCH that way, and I rather think I can manage her. But already she has warned me not to interfere with her young man! As if I would!"

Just here, Patty's cheeks grew red again, and she changed the subject of her epistolary progress.

"The baby is a perfect darling, and her parents are very nice people. TERRIBLY devoted to the infant, but of course that's to be expected. Roger is a comfort. It's so nice to have an old friend here among all these strangers. Oh, and there's an artist who, I know, spells his art with a big A. He wants to paint me as 'Cherry Ripe' or something, I forget what. But I know his portraits will look just like magazine covers. Though, - I suppose I AM rather of that type myself. Oh, me! I wish I were a tall, dark beauty, with melting brown eyes and midnight tresses, instead of a tow-headed, doll-faced thing. But then, as the poet says, 'We women cannot choose our lot.' I'm in for a good time, there's no doubt about that. We've parties and picnics and pageants piled up mountain high. So if I don't write again very soon, you'll know it's because I'm a Social Butterfly for the time being, and these are my Butterfly Days. Aunt Adelaide is rather nicer than when I last wrote. She gets on her 'company manners,' and that makes her more amiable."

"My goodness gracious!"

This last phrase was spoken aloud, not written, for the low, open window, near which Patty sat writing, was suddenly invaded by a laughing face and a pair of broad, burly shoulders, and Big Bill's big voice said, "Hello, you pretty little poppet!"

CHAPTER X

JUST A SHORT SPIN

Stop! Look! Listen!" cried Patty, gaily, as the unabashed intruder calmly seated himself on the broad, low window-sill. "Do you consider it good manners to present yourself in this burglarious fashion?"

"Well, you see, my room opens on this same veranda, - indeed the veranda seems to run all around the house on this story, - and so I thought I'd walk about a bit. Then I chanced to spy you, and - well, I'm still spying. Is this your dinky boudoir? How fussy it is."

"I like it so," said Patty, smiling.

"Of course you do. You're fussy yourself."

"I am not! I'm NOT fussy!"

"Oh, I don't mean that the way you think I do. I mean you're all dressed fussy, with pink ribbons and lace tassels and furbelows."

"Yes; I do love frilly clothes. Now, I suppose your ideal girl wears plain tailor-made suits, and stiff white collars, and small hats without much trimming, - just a band and a quill."

"Say, that's where you're 'way off! I like to see girls all dollied up in squffly lace over-skirts, - or whatever you call 'em, - with dinky little bows here and there."

"Is this frock all right, then?" asked Patty, demurely, knowing that her summer afternoon costume was of the very type he had tried to describe.

"Just the ticket! I'm not much on millinery, but you look like an apple blossom trimmed with sunshine."

"Why, you're a poet! Only poets talk like that. I doubt if Mr. Cromer could say anything prettier."

"'Tisn't pretty enough for you. Only a chap like Austin Dobson could make poetry about you."

The earnest sincerity in the big blue eyes of the Westerner robbed the words of any semblance of impertinence, and Patty spoke out her surprise.

"Why, do you read Austin Dobson? I never thought -"

She paused, lest she hurt his feelings by her implication, but Farnsworth went on, quietly:

"You never thought a big, hulking fellow like me could appreciate anything exquisite and dainty, either in poetry or in people," he said. "I don't blame you, Miss Fairfield; I am uncouth, uncultured, and unmannered. But I am fond of books, and, perhaps by the law of contrast, I am especially fond of the Minor Poets."

"You shan't call yourself those horrid names," said Patty, for his tones rang true, and she began to appreciate his honest nature; "no one can be uncouth or uncultured who loves such reading. Don't you love the big poets, too?"

"Yes; but I suppose everybody does that. I say, won't you come outside for a bit? That room is stuffy, and the air out here now is great. Couldn't you skip down with me for a whiff of the sea?"

"Why, I ought to be dressing for dinner."

"Oh, there's lots of time yet. Come on. Don't tell anybody, just fly out at this window, like Peter Pan, and we'll elope for half an hour."

Acting impulsively, Patty swung herself through the low window, and had descended the picturesque outside stairway that led from the upper veranda to the lower one before she remembered Daisy's prohibition.

"Oh, I think I won't go down to the beach," she said, suddenly pausing at the foot of the stairs. "I must go right back."

"Nothing of the sort," and Farnsworth grasped her arm and fairly marched her along the path to the gate. "You're not a quitter, I know, so what silly notion popped into your head just then?"

Patty laughed outright at his quick appreciation of her mood.

"Well," she parried, "you see, I don't know you very well."

"All the more reason for snatching this chance to get acquainted."

"Somebody might see us."

"Let them. It's no crime to stroll down to the beach."

"Somebody might object to my monopolising you like this."

"Who, Mona?"

"No; not Mona."

"Who, then?"

"Is there no one who might justly do so?"

"No, indeed! Unless Mrs. Parsons thinks I'm neglecting her."

"Nonsense. I don't mean her. But, what about Miss Dow?"

"Daisy Dow! Well, Miss Fairfield, I'm a blunt Westerner, and I don't know how to say these things subtly, but when you imply that Daisy has any special interest in me, you do me undeserved honour. I've known her for years, and we're good chums, but she'd have no right to comment if I walked down to the sea, or into it, or across it. NOW, will you be good?" They had reached the beach, and stood looking at the great rollers coming in, their white crests tinged by the last rays of the setting sun, which flashed a good-bye at them from the opposite horizon.

"It's fortunate you Eastern people have a sea," Farnsworth said, as he gazed across the black distance, "or you wouldn't know the meaning of the word space.

Your lives and living are so cramped."

"You Western people have a sea, too, I believe," said Patty.

"Yes, but we don't really need it, as you do. We have seas of land, rolling all over the place. We can get our breath inland; you have to come to the ocean to get a full breath."

"That's the popular superstition. I mean, that we are cramped and all that. But, really, I think we all have room enough. I think the Westerner's idea of wanting several acres to breathe in is just a habit."

Farnsworth looked at her steadily. "Perhaps you're right," he said; "at any rate, you seem to know all about it. Do you suppose I could learn to see it as you do?"

"Of course you could. But why should you? If you like the West, the big, breezy, long-distance West, there's no reason why you should cultivate a taste for our little cramped up, stuffy East."

"That's right! But I wish I could show you our country. Wouldn't you love to go galloping across a great prairie, - tearing ahead for illimitable miles, - breathing the air that has come, fresh and clean, straight down from the blue sky?"

"You make it sound well, but after that mad gallop is over, what then? A shack or ranch, or whatever you call it, with whitewashed walls, and rush mats and a smoky stove?"

"By George! You're about right! It wouldn't suit YOU, would it? You couldn't fit into that picture!"

"I'm 'fraid not. But if we're going to fit into the picture soon to assemble in Mona's dining-room, we must make a start in that direction. Mr. Farnsworth -"

"Call me Bill, oh, DO call me Bill!"

"Why should I?"

"Because I want you to; and because I think you might make that much concession to my Western primitiveness and unceremoniousness."

"But I don't like the name of Bill. It's so, - so -"

"So uncouth? Yes, it is. But I'm not the sort to be called William. Well, DO call me something pleasant and amiable."

"I'll call you Little Billee. That's Thackeray's, and therefore, it's all right. Now, can you slip me back into my own apartments as quietly as you took me away?"

"Of course I can, as it's nearly dark now. Here we go!"

He aided her up the stairs, and along the balcony to her own windows. Patty sprang lightly over the low sill, and waved her hand gaily as she pulled down her blinds and flashed on the electric lights. Then she rang for Janet, and found that a hurried toilette was necessary if she would be prompt at dinner.

One of Patty's prettiest evening frocks was a dainty French thing of white chiffon, decked with pale green ribbons and exquisite artificial apple blossoms made of satin. With a smile at the memory of Farnsworth's allusion to apple blossoms, she put it on, and twisted a wreath of the same lovely flowers in her golden crown of curls.

Then she danced downstairs to find the Western man awaiting her. He looked very handsome in evening clothes, and the easy unconsciousness of his pose and manner made him seem to Patty the most attractive man she had ever seen.

"I've arranged it with Mona," he said, straight-forwardly, "and I'm to take you in to dinner. I want to sit next to you."

But Patty had caught sight of Daisy Dow, and the angry gleam in that young woman's eyes warned Patty that Farnsworth's plan boded trouble.

Moreover, perverse Patty objected to being appropriated so calmly, and with a deliberate intent to pique Farnsworth, she replied, gaily:

"Nay, nay, fair sir; it suits me not, thus to be parcelled out. We Eastern girls are not to be had for the asking."

The smile she flashed at him brought an answering smile to Farnsworth's face, but as he stepped forward to urge her to grant his wish, Patty slipped her hand in Roger's arm, and joined the others who were already going to the dining-room.

She had quickly seen that this move on her part would leave Farnsworth no choice but to escort Daisy Dow, for Roger had been assigned to that fair maiden.

"What's up?" enquired Roger, as he obediently followed Patty's whispered order to "come along and behave yourself."

"Nothing," returned Patty, airily; "I have to have my own way, that's all; and as my old friend and comrade, you have to help me to get it."

"Always ready," declared Roger, promptly, "but seems to me, Pitty-Pat, the colossal cowboy is already a Willing Willy to your caprices."

"Don't be silly, Roger. He's so unused to our sort of society that he's willing to bow down at the shrine of any pretty girl."

"Oh, Patsy-Pat! Do you consider YOURSELF a pretty girl? How CAN you think so? Your nose turns up, and I think you're a little cross-eyed -"

"Oh, Roger, I am not!"

"Well, perhaps I'm mistaken about that; but you've a freckle on your left cheek, and a curl on your right temple is out of place."

"It isn't! I fixed it there on purpose! It's supposed to look coquettish."

"Very untidy!" and Roger glared in pretended disapproval at the curl that had purposely been allowed to escape from the apple-blossom wreath.

Patty liked Roger's fooling, for they were old chums and thoroughly good friends, and it was one of his customary jokes to pretend that he was trying to correct her tendency to personal vanity.

Beside the house party, there were several other guests, mostly Spring Beach cottagers, and the dinner was a gay one. Jack Pennington sat at Patty's other side, and Farnsworth and Daisy Dow were far away, near the head of the table.

"Dashing girl, Miss Dow," said Jack, as he looked at the vivacious Daisy, who was entertaining those near her with picturesque stories of Western life.

"Yes, indeed," said Patty; "and very clever and capable."

"Now, isn't it funny! Just from the way you say that, I know you don't like her."

Patty was dismayed. If she didn't altogether like Daisy, she had no wish to have other people aware of the fact.

"Oh, Jack, don't be mean. I DO like her."

"No, you don't; at least, not very much. She isn't your style."

"Well, then, if you think that, don't say it. I MUST like Mona's guests."

"Yes, of course. Forgive a poor, blundering idiot! And don't worry, Patty, no one shall ever know from me that you and the Dashing Daisy aren't boon companions."

"You're so nice and understanding, Jacky boy, and I'm much obliged. Do you remember the night you discovered who our chaperon was, and you helped me out so beautifully?"

"Always glad to help the ladies. What are we doing to-night, after this feast of fat things is over?"

"Nothing especial; dance a little, I suppose, sit around on the veranda, sing choruses, and that sort of thing."

"There's a glorious full moon. Couldn't we escape for a little spin? Just a very short one, in my runabout?"

"Yes, I'd love to. Or we could take my runabout."

"Or Mona's for that matter. I don't care what car we take, but I do love a short, quick drive, and then come back for the dance."

"All right, I'll go. Mona won't mind, if I don't stay long."

"Oh, only just around a block or two. Just to clear the effect of these flowers and candles from our brain."

"Isn't your brain a little weak, if it can't stand flowers and candles?" asked Patty, laughing.

"Perhaps it is, and perhaps that's only an excuse to get away. Hooray! Mona's rising now; let's make a mad dash."

"No; that isn't the way. Let's slide out quietly and inconspicuously, through this side door."

Adopting this idea, Jack and Patty went out on a side veranda, and stepped across the terrace to the garden paths. The moonlight turned the picturesque flower-beds to fairy fields, and Patty paused on one of the terrace landings.

"I don't know as I want to go motoring, Jack," she said, perching herself on the marble balustrade; "it's so lovely here."

"Just as you like, girlie. Ha! methinks I hear vocal speech! Some one approacheth!"

Farnsworth and Daisy Dow came strolling along the terrace, and Daisy took a seat beside Patty, while the two men stood in front of them.

"Won't you girls catch cold?" said Farnsworth, in his matter-of-fact way.

"These be not mortal maidens," said Jack, who was in whimsical mood. "These be two goddesses from Olympian heights, who have deigned to visit us for a brief hour."

"And unless you're very good to us," observed Patty, "we'll spread our wings and fly away."

"Let's do something," said Daisy, restlessly; "it's poky, just sitting here, doing nothing. I'd like to go in the ocean. It must be lovely to bounce around in the surf by moonlight."

"You'd bounce into bed with pneumonia," said Patty. "But Jack and I were talking of motoring. Suppose we take two runabouts and go for a short spin."

All agreed, and the quartette went to the garage for

Carolyn Wells

the cars.

The head chauffeur, who was not of an over kindly disposition, informed them that Miss Galbraith's run-about was out of commission for the moment, though Miss Fairfield's was in good shape.

"I'll get mine," proposed Jack, but Bill Farnsworth said, "No, I don't understand an electric awfully well. Let's take this car. I can run this O.K., and it will hold the four of us."

"All right," said Jack; "we're only going a few blocks up the beach. Hop in, Patty."

Farnsworth and Daisy sat in front, and Patty and Jack behind, and they started off at a brisk speed. The girls declined to go back to the house for wraps, as it was a warm evening, and the ride would be short. But when Farnsworth found himself with the wheel in his hand and a long stretch of hard, white road ahead of him, he forgot all else in the glory of the opportunity, and he let the car go at an astonishing speed.

"Isn't this fun!" cried Patty, but the words were fairly blown away from her lips as they dashed along.

"This is the way we Westerners ride!" exclaimed Daisy, as she sat upright beside Bill, her hair streaming back from her forehead, the light scarf she wore round her neck flapping back into Patty's face.

"It's grand!" gasped Jack. "But I hope Big Bill knows what he's about."

"You bet he does!" replied Bill himself, and they

whizzed on.

Patty had never gone so fast. Though it was a warm night, the rush of wind chilled her, and she shivered. Jack, seeing this, picked up a lap-robe and wrapped it about her.

"Don't want to turn back yet, do you?" he asked.

"We must turn soon," Patty managed to reply, but Jack scarcely heard the words.

The big moon was setting when Bill turned the car inland, and shouting, "We're going to drive straight into that moon!" made a mad dash toward it.

"Hurry up!" cried Patty. "Catch it before it drops below the horizon. Speed her!"

CHAPTER XI

THE WORST STORM EVER!

Patty's gay words added the final spur to Farnsworth's enthusiasm, and with a whoop of glee, he darted ahead faster than ever. Though his manner and appearance gave the effect of recklessness, Big Bill knew quite well what he was doing. He was a magnificent driver, and however seemingly careless he might be, his whole mind was alert and intent on his work. The road, hard and white, glistened in the moonlight. Straight and clear, it seemed truly to lead directly into the great yellow disk, now dropped almost low enough to touch it.

"Whoopee!" shouted Bill. "This is some going! Sit tight, Daisy, and hold on for all you're worth! Are you people in the back hall all right?"

"Right we are!" returned Jack. "Are you going straight THROUGH the moon?"

"Yep! If we catch her in time! Hallo, she's touched the earth!"

It was a great game. The road was so level and so free of obstruction that they kept the centre, and seemed to be shooting, at whistling speed, into that enormous yellow circle.

But, already, the horizon was swallowing up their goal. The laughing quartette saw the circle of gold become a semi-circle, then a mere arc, and soon only a glimpse of yellow remained, which immediately vanished, and save for a faint reminiscent glow, the western sky was dark.

"Where are your stars?" queried Farnsworth, gazing upward. "Nice country, this! No stars, no moon, no nothin'!"

"The lamps give enough light," cried Daisy. "Don't slow down, Bill! Go on, this flying is grand!"

"Come on in, - the flying's fine!" laughed Bill, and again they went at highest speed.

But with the setting of the moon, Patty's spirit of adventure calmed down.

"Oh, do let's turn back," she begged. "He doesn't hear me, - make him hear, Jack."

"I say, Farnsworth," and Jack tapped the burly shoulder in front of him, "we've gone far enough. Back to the old home, eh?"

"Back it is!" and the driver slowed down, and picking a wide, clear space, deftly turned the machine around. But at sight of the eastern sky, every one exclaimed in dismay.

Though the moon had set clearly, and the west was a dull grey, the eastern sky was black. Turbulent masses of clouds climbed, rolling, to the zenith; faint lights appeared now and then, and a dim rumble of distant thunder was heard at intervals.

"Shower coming up," said Farnsworth, blithely; "better streak for home. Wish I'd turned sooner. But we'll beat the storm. Wish the girls had some wraps. Here, Daisy, take my coat and put it on while you've a chance. It'll look pretty silly on you, but it will keep your furbelows from getting spoiled."

"Yes, I will take it, Billy. I'm awfully chilly."

As Daisy already had a laprobe, Patty looked at her in astonishment, as she let Farnsworth take off his coat and put it on her. An ordinary evening coat, it was not a great protection, but Daisy turned up the collar and made herself as comfortable as she could. Then she tucked the laprobe carefully over her skirts, though as yet no drop of rain had descended.

"No, indeed!" said Patty, as Jack offered her his coat. "I have the laprobe, you know, and I'll put it round my shoulders. Never mind if my skirts are spoilt. Turn up your collar, Jack, it will pour in a minute now."

And pour it did! Suddenly, without a preliminary sprinkle, the floods dropped straight from the heavens. A drenching, pouring rain that soaked the occupants of the open car before they could realise what had happened. Gusts of wind added to their discomfort, and then the thunder and lightning, drawn nearer, gave the greatest exhibition of an electrical storm that had been seen all summer.

Patty, who was confessedly afraid of thunder storms,

shivered, on the verge of nervous hysterics. Finally, at a specially ear-splitting bolt and blinding flash, which were almost simultaneous, she gave a little shriek and pulled the wet laprobe over her head. She crumpled down into a little heap, and, frightened lest she should faint, Pennington put his arm round her and held her in a reassuring clasp.

Daisy Dow was more angry than frightened. She hadn't Patty's fear of the elements, but she greatly objected to the uncomfortable situation in which she found herself.

"Do get home, Bill!" she cried, crossly. "Can't you go any faster?"

The big fellow, in his white shirtsleeves, bent to his wheel. He had worn no hat, and the rain fairly rebounded as it dashed on his thick mat of soaking wet hair.

"Speed her, Bill," went on Daisy, petulantly; "you could go fast enough in the moonlight, - why do you slow down now, when we all want to get home?"

No answer from Farnsworth, who was intently looking and listening.

"Why DO you, Bill?" reiterated the irritating voice, and Farnsworth's never very patient temper gave way.

"Shut up, Daisy!" he cried. "I'm doing the best I can, - but that's all the good it does. We've got to stop. The gasolene is out!"

All of them, accustomed to motors, knew what this meant. Like a flash, each mind flew back to think who was to blame for this. And each realised that it was not the fault of the chauffeur at "Red Chimneys" who had let them take out the car. For, had they not said they were going only for a short spin? And the car had been amply stocked for about two hours. Yes, it must be about two hours since they started, for in their merry mood they had had no thought of time, and had gone far, far inland.

"We can't stop," shrieked Daisy, "in this storm! No house or shelter near! Bill Farnsworth, I'll NEVER forgive you for bringing me into this pickle!"

Farnsworth gave a short, sharp laugh.

"I can get along without your forgiveness, Daisy, if I can only get you people home safely. Great Cats, how it rains! I say, Pennington, what do you think we'd better do? Where's Miss Fairfield?"

Looking around suddenly, Bill saw no sign of Patty in the nondescript heap by Jack's side. But at his startled question, a wet face and a mass of tangled curls and apple blossoms, equally wet, emerged from the soaking laprobe.

"Here I am!" said a plaintive little voice that tried hard to be brave. But a sharp flare of lightning sent the golden head suddenly back to its hiding-place.

"Miss Fairfield is awfully afraid of electrical storms," explained Jack, patting the wet heap anywhere, in a well-meant attempt at reassurance.

"Pooh!" exclaimed Daisy. "What a 'fraid-cat! I'm not frightened, - but I' terribly wet. I'm soaked!

I'm drowned!"

"So are we all, Daisy," said Bill, shivering as the wind flapped his dripping shirtsleeves; "but what CAN we do? The car won't move."

"Well, WE can move! Let's get out and walk."

"Why, Daisy, what's the use? Where could we walk to?"

"Well, I think you two men are horrid! You just sit there and let Patty and me catch our death of cold. Though Patty is wrapped up snug and warm in that robe. If SHE'S protected you don't care about ME!"

"Daisy! what nonsense -" began Bill, but Patty's head popped out again.

"If you think I'm snug and warm, Daisy Dow, you're greatly mistaken! I NEVER was so uncomfortable in all my life! And I'm scared besides! That's more than you are!"

Jack Pennington laughed. "While the girls are comparing notes of discomfort," he said, "how about us, Bill? Do you feel,-er - well-groomed and all that?"

Farnsworth looked critically at his soaked apparel. "I've been DRIER," he replied, "but you know, Pennington, I'm one of those chaps who look well in any costume!"

The absurdity of this speech brought Patty's head out again, and she felt a shock of surprise to note that the jesting words were true. Bill Farnsworth, coatless, dripping wet, and exceedingly uncomfortable, sat upright, tossing back his clustered wet hair, and positively laughing at the situation.

"Pardon my hilarity," he said, as he caught a glimpse of Patty's face, "but you're all so lugubrious, somebody MUST laugh."

"All right, I'll laugh with you!" and Patty sat upright, the dark laprobe held hoodwise, so that she looked like a mischievous nun. "If you'll please turn off the thunder and lightning, I won't mind the rain a bit. In fact, I'm getting used to it. I know I was meant for a duck, anyway."

"Well, Duck, the thunder and lightning are getting farther away," said Bill, truly, "but I do believe it rains harder than ever! What CAN we do?"

"Can't we get under the car?" suggested Daisy.

"Not very well; and it wouldn't help much. It's rather wet, even under there," and Bill looked at the soaked road.

"We passed a house about a mile back," said Patty, "couldn't we walk back to that?"

"I thought of that," said Bill, "but I didn't suppose you girls could walk it, - with those foolish step-ladder heels you're wearing. And white satin slippers aren't real good style for mud-wading. I could carry you, Miss Fairfield, - you're only a will-o'-the-wisp; but Daisy here is a heavyweight."

"Oh, no matter about me," said Daisy, spitefully; "just

see that Miss Fairfield is looked after!"

Big Bill Farnsworth looked at the speaker. "Daisy Dow," he said, quietly, "don't you get me any more riled than I am! If you do, I won't be pleasant!"

"But I can walk," put in Patty, anxious to prevent a quarrel. "I haven't on walking boots exactly, but I can flounder along somehow. And we MUST get to shelter! Help me along, Jack, and I'll try not to mind the thunder and lightning."

"Plucky little girl!" said Farnsworth, and Daisy scowled in the darkness.

"What time is it?" asked Patty, who was now thoroughly ready to face the situation.

"Just twelve o'clock," replied Jack, after several futile attempts to light a match and see his watch.

"Then we MUST try to get to that house," declared Patty. "I had no idea it was so late. Come, people, no matter what the result, we must TRY to reach shelter and civilisation."

"Right!" said Pennington. "It's the only thing to do. I remember the house. There was no light in it, though."

"No; it's so late. But we can ring up the family, and they'll surely take us in for the night."

"Not if they see us first!" exclaimed Bill. "Oh, Miss Fairfield, you look like Ophelia with those flowers tumbling all over your face!"

Carolyn Wells

Patty laughed, and removing the apple-blossom wreath from her head, was about to throw it away. But she felt it gently taken from her hand in the darkness, and she somehow divined that Farnsworth had put it in his pocket.

The combination of this sentimental act with the drenched condition of the flower wreath - and, presumably, the pocket, was too much for Patty, and she giggled outright.

"What ARE you laughing at?" snapped Daisy. "*I* don't see anything funny in this whole performance."

"Oh, DO think it's funny, Daisy," implored Patty, still laughing. "Oh, DO! for it ISN'T funny at all, unless we MAKE it so by thinking it IS so!"

"Stop talking nonsense," Daisy flung back. "Oh, I've sprained my ankle. I can't walk at all! Oh, oh!"

Farnsworth looked at her. "Daisy," he said, sternly, "if you've really sprained your ankle, we'll have to get back into the car - for I can't carry you. But if you CAN walk, I advise you to do so."

Daisy looked a little frightened at his severe tone.

"Oh, I suppose I CAN walk," she said, "though it hurts me dreadfully. Hold me up, Bill."

"I'll hold you," he replied, cheerily. "Now we'll take this lantern, and we'll walk ahead. Pennington, you follow with Miss Fairfield. Don't talk much, you'll need all your strength to walk through the storm. It's abating a little, but it's raining cats and dogs yet."

Unconsciously, Bill had assumed command of the expedition, and involuntarily, the others obeyed him. That mile was a dreadful walk! At first, it seemed fairly easy, for the road was a good one, though wet and slippery. But soon the satin slippers were soaked; stones and bits of gravel made their way inside, and at last Patty found it almost impossible to keep hers on at all. Jack tried to help, by tying the little slippers on with his own and Patty's handkerchiefs, but these soon gave way. The rain fell steadily now; not in dashes and sheets, but a moderate downpour that seemed as if it meant to go on forever.

Jack could do little to help, save to grasp Patty's arm tightly and "boost" her along. Daisy stood it better, for she was of far stronger build than fragile Patty, and Big Bill almost carried her along with his own long, sturdy strides.

After what seemed an interminable walk, they reached the house in question. It was a large, fine-looking structure, but as no lights were visible, the family had evidently retired.

"I should think they'd leave a night light in the hall," grumbled Daisy, as the quartette climbed the veranda steps and stood, dripping, at the front door.

"Whew!" exclaimed Jack. "It's good to get where that rain doesn't drive straight into your eyes, anyway! Ring the bell, Farnsworth."

"Can't find it. Ah, here it is!" and Bill pushed the electric button, and held it, ringing a continuous peal.

But no one came to the door, and the shivering four

grew impatient, to think that shelter was so near, yet unavailable.

"You keep punching this bell, Pennington," suggested Bill, "and I'll reconnoitre round to the other entrances. There must be side doors and things."

Jack kept the bell going, but no one responded, and no lights showed in the house. At last Bill returned from his tour of exploration.

"I've been all the way round," he said; "there are three or four entrances to this mansion, and all have bells, but nobody answered my various and insistent ringings. WHAT shall us do now, poor things?"

"I suppose they're afraid we're burglars," observed Patty; "and they're afraid to let us in."

"If they don't come pretty soon, I WILL be a burglar," declared Bill, "and I'll get in in burglar fashion. It isn't fair for people to have a warm, dry house, and keep forlorn wet people out of it. We've GOT to get in! Let's bang on the doors."

But no amount of banging and pounding, no shaking of door knobs, no whistling or shouting served to bring response.

"Throw pebbles at the window," Patty suggested, and immediately a young hailstorm bombarded the second-story panes.

"No good!" commented Bill. "So here goes!" and without further warning his large and well-aimed foot crashed through a long front window which reached down to the floor.

"Oh, my gracious!" exclaimed Patty. "WHAT a thing to do!"

"The only way is the best way," returned Bill, gaily. "Now, wait a minute, you girls, I'll let you in."

Carefully looking out for the broken glass, Big Bill inserted his hand, sprung back the catch, and opened the window.

"Don't come in this way," he cautioned, "I'll open the front door."

Farnsworth found himself in a large, pleasant room, evidently a drawing-room. But without pausing to look around, he made for the hall, and tried to open the great front doors.

"Can't do it," he called to those outside. "I'll open another window."

In a moment, he had thrown up the sash of another long, low window, in a room the other side of the hall, and invited his friends in.

"Couldn't let you girls walk in on that broken glass," he explained. "Come in this way, and make yourselves at home."

"We're too wet, - we'll spoil things," said Patty, hesitating at the long lace curtains and fine floors and rugs.

"Nonsense! Come on! Where DO you suppose the

electric light key is? Whoo! here we have it!"

A flood of light filled the room, and the girls saw they were in a comfortable, pleasant library or sitting-room, evidently the home of cultured, refined people.

CHAPTER XII

A WELCOME SHELTER

A piano stood open, and Daisy sat at it, striking a few chords of "Home, Sweet Home."

This made them all laugh, but Farnsworth said, reprovingly, "Come away from that, Daisy. We have to enter this house to shelter ourselves, but we needn't spoil their belongings unnecessarily."

Daisy pouted, but she came away from the piano, having already left many drops of water on its keys and shining rosewood case.

Patty smiled appreciatively at Bill's thoughtfulness, but said, with growing alarm:

"Where DO you suppose the people are? They MUST have heard us come in, even if they were sound asleep."

"It's pretty queer, I think," said Jack.

"Oh!" cried Daisy, "what do you mean? Do you think there's anything WRONG?" and she began to cry, in sheer, hysterical fright and discomfort.

"It IS queer," agreed Bill, looking out into the hall, and listening.

Then Patty's practical good sense came to her aid.

"Nonsense!" she said. "You're an ungrateful bunch! Here you have shelter from the storm, and you all begin to cry! Well, no," she added, smiling, "you boys are not exactly crying, - but if you were girls, you WOULD be! Now, behave yourselves, and brace up to this occasion! First, there's a fireplace, and here's a full woodbox. Build a roaring fire, and let's dry off a little. Meantime, I wish you two men would go over the house, and find out who's in it. Daisy and I will stay here."

"*I* won't stay here alone with Patty," sobbed Daisy, who was shaking with nervous fear.

"There, there, Daisy," said Bill, "don't cry. I'll fix it. Miss Fairfield, you're a brick! Your ideas, as I shall amend them, are fine! Pennington, you stay here with the girls, and build the biggest fire you can make. I'll investigate this domicile, and see if the family are really the Seven Sleepers, or if they're surely afraid to come downstairs, for fear we're burglars."

Patty flashed a glance of admiration at the big fellow, but she only said:

"Go along, Little Billee; but hurry back and dry yourself before you catch pneumonia."

Bill went off whistling, and Jack and Patty built a rousing fire. The woodbox was ample and well filled, and the fireplace, a wide one, and the crackling flames felt most grateful to the wet refugees. Jack wanted to go after Farnsworth, but Daisy wouldn't hear of it, so he stayed with the girls. Soon Big Bill returned, smiling all over his good-natured face.

"Not a soul in the whole house!" he reported. "I've been all over it, from attic to cellar. Everything in good order; beds made up, and so forth. But no food in the larder, so I assume the family has gone away for a time."

"Well, of all funny situations!" exclaimed Patty. Cheered by the warmth, her face was smiling and dimpling, and her drying hair was curling in soft tendrils all over her head.

"Come to the fire, Little Billee, and see if you can't begin to commence to dry out a little bit."

"I've just washed my hair, and I can't do a thing with it!" said Big Bill, comically, as he ran his fingers through his thick mane of brown, wavy hair. "But, I say, this fire feels good! Wow! But I'm damp! I say, Pennington, I've been thinking."

"Hard?"

"Yes, hard. Now you must all listen to me. I expect opposition, but it doesn't matter. What I'm going to say now, GOES! See?"

Bill looked almost ferocious in his earnestness, and Patty looked at him with admiration. He was so big and powerful, physically, and now his determined face and strongly set jaw betokened an equal mental power. "I'm at the head of this expedition, and in the present

Carolyn Wells

emergency, my word is law!" He banged his clenched fist on the mantel, as he stood before the fire, and seemed fairly to challenge a reply.

"Well, go on," said Patty, laughing. "What's it all about?"

"It's just this. You two girls have got to stay in this house, ALONE, while Pennington and I walk back to Spring Beach, NOW! '

"Good gracious! What for?" exclaimed

Patty, while Daisy screamed, "I WON'T do it! I WON'T stay here alone!"

"Be quiet," said Bill, looking at Daisy sternly. "You MUST do as I say."

"You're right, Farnsworth," said Jack Pennington. "It's nearly one o'clock, and we must start right off."

"Yes," agreed Bill. "Now, Miss Fairfield, I assure you, you will be perfectly safe here. It isn't a pleasant prospect, but there's nothing else to be done. The house is securely fastened against intruders. You can lock the drawing-room doors on this side, so the broken window need cause you no uneasiness. We will walk back to 'Red Chimneys,' unless we can get a lift somehow. But, at any rate, we will send a car back here for you at the earliest possible moment."

"It IS the only thing to do," agreed Patty; "but I hate to have you boys start out so wet. Can't you borrow from your host's wardrobe?"

"Good idea!" laughed Bill. "I saw some men's raincoats in the hall. I think we will appropriate them, eh, Pennington?"

With very few further words, the two men took possession of raincoats, rubbers, and umbrellas belonging to their unknown hosts, and went out through the open, broken window into the night. It was still raining, but not so hard, and Bill called back cheerily, "Good-night, ladies," as they tramped away.

"It's awful," Daisy whimpered, "to leave us two girls here alone and unprotected! I know we'll be robbed and murdered by highwaymen!"

"You're talking nonsense, Daisy," said Patty, sternly. "Now, look here, if you'll just be friendly and decent, we needn't have such a bad time, but if you're going to be cross and cry all the time, I shall simply let you alone, and we'll have a horrid, uncomfortable time."

This straightforward, common-sense talk brought Daisy to her senses, and though she still looked petulant, she made no more cross or unkind speeches.

"What are you going to do?" she enquired as Patty took off her chiffon gown, and held it carefully before the fire. "That frock is ruined."

"Yes, I know, but I'm going to pick it out and make it look as decent as I can. I suppose I'll have to wear it home when I go. Take off yours, and I'll dry them both nicely. I'm good at this sort of thing. Here, I'll unhook it."

Daisy dropped her own party frock on the floor and

showed little interest as Patty picked it up and daintily fingered its frills into something like shapeliness.

"Hunt around, Daisy,' Patty said, knowing it best to keep the girl occupied. "Surely you can find something to put round our shoulders. An afghan or even a table cover would do for a dressing jacket."

Slightly interested, Daisy went into the next room and returned with two lengths of brocaded silk.

"They're bookcase curtains," she explained. "I slipped the rings off the pole. See, we can each have one."

"Good!" said Patty, draping the curtain round her shoulders, sontag fashion. "These are fine. Now, see, I'm getting your dress quite fluffy again."

"So you are. I'll finish it, and you do your own. Aren't you going to bed, Patty?"

"No, not exactly. Suppose we sleep here. You take the couch, and I'll doze in this big armchair."

"Are you - are you frightened, Patty?"

"N - no; NO! Of course I'm not! What's there to be afraid of?"

"Well - I am," and Daisy began to whimper, and then to cry.

"Daisy Dow! You stop that! I'd be all right if you'd behave yourself! Now, don't you get hysterical! If you do, I'll - I'll telephone for the doctor! Oh, Daisy! the TELEPHONE! WHY didn't we think of that before?

There MUST be one! Let's hunt for it."

Spurred by this new thought, Patty ran through the rooms in search of a telephone. She found one in the back part of the hall, but, alas, it had been disconnected and was useless.

"Bill must have found that out," Patty said, thoughtfully; "and he didn't tell us."

"Why not?" demanded Daisy. "Why wouldn't he tell us?"

"Because he's so thoughtful and considerate. I feel sure he thought it would make us feel more lonely if we knew the telephone was there, but wouldn't work."

"Well, it does!" declared Daisy. "I'm so lonely and frightened and miserable, I believe I'll die!"

"Oh, no, you won't," said Patty, cheerfully. "Now, I'll tell you what, Daisy. You lie down on the couch, - here's a nice afghan to put over you, - and I'll sing a little."

This sounded comfortable, so Daisy, now quite warm and dry, lay down, and after tucking the afghan over her, Patty went to the piano. She played a few soft chords, and then sang, softly, a crooning lullaby. It is not surprising that under the influence of the soothing music, the warm fire, and her own fatigue, Daisy soon fell sound asleep.

Assured of this, Patty left the piano, and sat in the big easy-chair in front of the fire. She thought over their escapade, and though it was certainly serious enough, she smiled to herself as she thought of the humorous side of it. It certainly seemed funny for Daisy and herself to be alone in a big, handsome, strange house, - wrapped in other people's bookcase curtains! Then she thought of Big Bill and Jack trudging miles and miles through the storm. What a splendid fellow Bill Farnsworth was, anyhow! He had left no room for argument or even discussion; he had decided there was but one way out of this situation, and he took it. Jack had acquiesced, and had done as he was told, but Bill had been the moving spirit. What good sense he had shown! And with what forgetfulness of self he had accepted his own hard part of the performance. Of course the boys wouldn't have to walk all the way to Spring Beach. Of course they would manage somehow to get a conveyance, but Bill had not bothered about such details; he had seen his way, and had walked straight out into it. Surely he was a splendid man, - a big, fine man, - and - he had taken her apple-blossom wreath, - and he had put it in his pocket, - because - because -

And even as she thought of Bill's confiscation of her flowers, Patty's golden head drooped a little, the long lashes fell over her blue eyes, and in the sheltering depths of the soft-cushioned chair, she fell sound asleep.

A few hours later she awoke. At first she couldn't realise where she was, then, like a flash, the truth came to her. Greatly refreshed by her nap, she jumped up, smiling.

The fire was out, so she rekindled it, and proceeded to don her dried but sadly wilted looking party dress. She hesitated a moment, and then concluded to wake

Daisy, as a rescuing party might arrive at any minute.

Daisy sat up on her couch, and rubbed her eyes. "What time is it?" she asked, not yet fully awake.

"I've no idea," said Patty, laughing. "I never wear my watch in the evening. But," and she looked from the window as she raised the blind, "I see streaks of pink, so that must be the east, and the sun is about ready to rise. So up, up, Lucy, the sun is in the sky, or will be soon. And I'm sure our deliverers will soon come to rescue us from this durance vile!"

Patty was in high spirits now, and danced about the room while she urged Daisy to get into her frock.

"Bookcase curtains are all very well for boudoir jackets," she said, "but not fit for appearance in polite society. See, your frock looks fairly well; a lot better than mine."

Sure enough the soft silk of Daisy's gown had stood its wetting much better than Patty's chiffon, but they were both sad wrecks of the dainty costumes they had been the evening before.

Patty flung open the windows, and let in the cool morning air, and as she stepped out on the veranda she cried, "Oh, Daisy, here they come!"

A big touring car was visible at a distance, and in a moment Patty saw that Farnsworth himself was driving it.

"Hooray!" he called, as he came nearer, and Mona, who sat beside him, cried out, "Oh, Patty, Patty! Are you safe?"

"Safe? Of course I'm safe," said Patty, who despite her draggled dress, looked like the incarnation of morning as she stood on the veranda, her sweet face glad and smiling beneath its cloud of golden curls.

"Thank Heaven!" cried Big Bill, as he fairly flung himself out of his driver's seat and rushed up to her. He almost took her in his arms, but just checked his mad impulse in time, and grasping both her hands, shook them vigorously up and down as he whispered, "Oh, my little girl! You never can know what it cost me to go off and leave you here alone!" His frank, honest blue eyes looked straight into her deep violet ones, and his glance told eloquently of his remorse and regret for the mischief he had thoughtlessly brought about.

Patty understood at once all his unspoken message, and smiled a full and free forgiveness.

"It's all right, Little Billee," she said, softly. "You were a brave, true friend, and I shall never forget your chivalry and true kindness."

A moment more he held her hands, gazing deep into her eyes, and then turned abruptly to greet Daisy.

CHAPTER XIII

AT DAISY'S DICTATION

At Farnsworth's directions, the "rescuing party" had brought with them a glazier and his kit of tools and materials. While he fitted a new pane of glass in place of the broken one, Mona expressed her opinion of the escapade of the night before.

"It was all your fault, Bill!" she exclaimed. "You ought not to have driven so fast and so far."

"I know it, ma'am," said Big Bill, looking like a culprit schoolboy. "I'm awful 'shamed of myself!"

"And well you may be!" chimed in Adele Kenerley. "Suppose this house hadn't been here, what would you have done?"

"I should have built one," declared Bill, promptly.

"So you would!" agreed Patty, heartily.

"You're equal to any emergency, Little Billee; and it WASN'T all your fault, anyway. *I* egged you on, because I love to drive fast, especially at night."

"Very reprehensible tastes, young woman," said Jim

Kenerley, trying to be severe, but not succeeding very well.

"Oh, you might have known this house was here," said Mona. "It's Mr. Kemper's house. They've gone away for a month. They're coming back next week."

"Well, they'll find everything in order," said Patty. "We didn't hurt a thing, except the window, and we've fixed that. We burned up a lot of their firewood, though."

"They won't mind that," said Mona, laughing. "They're awfully nice people. We'll come over and tell them the whole story when they get home."

"And now, can't we go home?" said Patty. "I'm just about starved."

"You poor dear child," cried Mrs. Kenerley. "You haven't had a bite of breakfast! Come on, Mona, let's take Patty and Daisy home in one of the cars; the rest can follow in the other."

Two cars of people had come over to escort the wanderers home, so this plan was agreed upon.

But somehow, Bill Farnsworth managed to hasten the glazier's task, so that all were ready to depart at once.

"I'll drive the big car," cried Bill. "Come on, Patty," and before any one realised it, he had swung the girl up into the front seat of the big touring car, and had himself climbed to the driver's seat.

"I had to do this," he said to Patty, as they started off.

"I must speak to you alone a minute, and be sure that you forgive me for the trouble I made you."

"Of course I forgive you," said Patty, gaily. "I'd forgive you a lot more than that."

"You would? Why?"

"Oh, because I'm such a good forgiver. I'd forgive anybody, anything."

"Huh! then it isn't much of a compliment to have YOUR forgiveness!"

"Well, why should I pay you compliments?"

"That's so! Why SHOULD you? In fact, it ought to be the other way. Let ME pay them to YOU."

"Oh, I don't care much about them. I get quite a lot, you see -"

"I see you're a spoiled baby, that's what YOU are!"

"Now, - Little Billee!" and Patty's tone was cajoling, and her sideways glance and smile very provoking.

"And I'd like to do my share of the spoiling!" he continued, looking at her laughing, dimpled face and wind-tossed curls.

"So you shall! Begin just as soon as you like and spoil me all you can," said Patty, still in gay fooling, when she suddenly remembered Daisy's prohibition of this sort of fun.

"Of course I don't mean all this," she said, suddenly speaking in a matter-cf-fact tone.

"But I do, and I shall hold you to it. You know I have your blossom wreath; I've saved it as a souvenir of last night."

"That forlorn bit of drowned finery! Oh, Little Billee, I thought you were poetical! No poet could keep such a tawdry old souvenir as that!"

"It isn't tawdry. I dried it carefully, and picked the little petals all out straight, and it's really lovely."

"Then if it's in such good shape, I wish you'd give it back to me to wear. I was fond of that wreath."

"No, it's mine now. I claim right of salvage. But I'll give you another in place of it, - if I may."

Patty didn't answer this, for Daisy, tired of being neglected, leaned her head over between the two, and commenced chattering.

The two girls were well wrapped up in coats and veils Mona had brought them, but they were both glad when they came in sight of "Red Chimneys."

Patty went gaily off to her own rooms, saying she was going to have a bath and a breakfast, and then she was going to sleep for twenty-four hours.

"I'm not," announced Daisy. "I'm going to make a straight dive for the breakfast room. Come with me, Bill, and see that I get enough to eat."

Roger, Mona, and the Kenerleys were going for an ocean dip, and Laurence Cromer, who was a late riser, had not yet put in an appearance. Aunt Adelaide was with Patty, hearing all about the adventure, so Bill was obliged to accept Daisy's rather peremptory invitation.

"What's the matter with you, Bill?" asked the girl, as she threw off her motor coat and sat at the table in her low-necked party gown.

"Nothing. I say, Daisy, why don't you go and get into some togs more suitable for 9 A.M.?"

"Because I'm hungry. Yes, James, omelet, and some of the fried chicken. Bill, don't you like me any more?"

"Yes, of course I do. But you ought to act more, - more polite, you know."

"Oh, fiddlesticks! You mean more finicky, - like that paragon, Patty. You think she's perfect, because she never raises her voice above a certain pitch, and she expects all you men to lie down and let her walk over you."

"She MAY walk over me, if she likes; and I want you to stop speaking of her in that slighting way, Daisy."

"Oh, you do, do you? And, pray, what right have you to say HOW I shall speak of her?"

"The right that any man has, to take the part of one who is absent."

"You'd like to have more rights than that, wouldn't you?"

"Maybe I would, but I'm not confiding in you."

"You don't have to. Yours is an open secret. Everybody can see you're perfectly gone on that little pink and white thing!"

"That will do, Daisy, don't say another word of that sort!" and Bill's voice was so stern and tense that Daisy stopped, a little frightened at his demeanour.

What he might have said further, she never knew, for just then Guy Martin and Lora Sayre came strolling into the room.

"Hello, people!" said Guy. "Where's everybody that belongs to this chateau? We've come through myriads of empty rooms, but at last we find the gems of the collection."

"Why, Miss Dow," exclaimed Lora, looking at Daisy's gown, "is this a DINNER party?"

Daisy laughed, and explained, rather pleased than otherwise to be the sole narrator of the interesting tale. Needless to say, she and Bill Farnsworth figured as the principal actors in her dramatic version of the motor adventure, and, naturally, Bill could not contradict her.

"I congratulate you, Miss Dow," said Guy, "on looking so fit after such a trying ordeal. Patty is all right, isn't she?"

"Oh, yes; she's all right, but you know, she can't stand much fatigue. And the whole performance unnerved her, and gave her a chance to insist on having a beauty sleep."

"Which she doesn't need for THAT purpose," laughed Lora, good-naturedly. "But I fear we are keeping you, Miss Dow. Don't you want to get into a morning frock? Wouldn't you feel more comfortable?"

"No, it doesn't matter," and Daisy's manner gave the effect of sacrificing her comfort to the guests, though really she was of no mind to run away and lose this call.

"We came to talk about the Pageant," began Guy. "We want to get the various parts settled."

"Well, of course we can't answer for the others," said Daisy, "but let's discuss it, - it's such fun, and among us, we may think up some good ideas. I've had lots of experience with this sort of thing out West."

"Oh, have you?" said Guy, eagerly. "Then DO help me out. I have to get up such a lot of characters, - all representative of the sea, you know. I want Mr. Farnsworth here for Father Neptune, that's certain."

"I'm quite willing," said Bill, good-naturedly. "Do I wear a bathing suit?"

"No, indeed," replied Lora. "You wear a gorgeous robe, all dark green muslin, in billowy waves, and cotton wool on it for sea foam. Then you'll have a stunning crown and a trident and a lot of paraphernalia."

"Lovely," said Bill. "I do think I'll look just sweet! Who is with me in this misery?"

"Well, the Spirit of the Sea is the next most important

figure on this float. I wanted to be it, but mother thinks I'm not strong enough to stand it. She refuses to let me try. So I suppose it will be Patty."

"Patty Fairfield!" exclaimed Daisy. "She's not strong enough, either. Suppose I take that part. I'm used to posing, and I can stand in one position without getting tired. I'll do it, if you want me to."

"But we've really asked Patty," demurred Guy, "and she hasn't decided yet."

"Well, leave it to me," said Daisy. "I'll ask her, and if she wants the part, all right, and if not, I'll take it."

This seemed satisfactory, and the matter was dropped while they discussed other details of the float.

Laurence Cromer came down while they were talking, and they all adjourned to the veranda, while the artist gave them the benefit of his advice as to decorations and scenic effects.

Then the bathers came back from the beach, and all went to work heartily to make and carry out plans for the Pageant.

Patty had luncheon sent to her room, for she was more affected by the exposure to the storm and the nerve exhaustion of the adventure than the others were. However, as Mona and Mrs. Kenerley and Baby May spent much of the time with her, she did not have a dull day. In the afternoon Daisy came in. Patty, in a blue silk negligee, sat at her desk writing letters.

"How sweet you look!" said Daisy, sitting beside her.

"When are you coming downstairs? The boys are moping all over the place. I believe you're staying up here for coquetry."

The tone was light, but Patty could see that Daisy's words were at least partly in earnest. But they were untrue, and Patty said, "Oh, I'm going down for tea. I'm just writing to my father. Then I'll dress and go downstairs. I'm all right, you know."

"Yes, you look so," said Daisy, glancing at the bright eyes and roseleaf complexion. "You don't look a bit tired."

"I'm not now; but I was when I reached home this morning. Weren't you?"

"Not very. I'm stronger than you are. Guy Martin and Lora Sayre were here to talk about the Pageant."

"Were they? Is Lora going to be Spirit of the Sea?"

"No; her mother won't let her. They asked me to take the part, but I don't want to."

"Why not?" said Patty, looking at her curiously.

"Oh, I think they'd better have a Spring Beach girl. You, for instance."

"They asked me before, but if you'll do it, I'll take something else. Who's going to be Neptune?"

"Bill. That's another reason why you'd better be the Sea Spirit."

"Nonsense!" and Patty was angry at herself to feel the blush that rose to her cheek. But Daisy made no comment, and in a moment she said suddenly:

"Patty, write a note for me, will you? I've run a sliver into my forefinger and I can't hold a pen."

"A sliver? Oh, Daisy, does it hurt?"

"No, not much now. I got it out. But the tip of my finger is painful if I write. You've your pen in your hand, so just scribble a line for me. I can sign it."

"Of course I will. Dictate, please!"

Patty took a fresh sheet of paper, and tried to look like a professional amanuensis.

"I really would rather not be the Spirit of the Sea," dictated Daisy, and Patty wrote obediently. "Please try to get some one else for the part. But may I ask you as a personal favour not to speak of the matter to me at any time."

"Thank you,' said Daisy, taking the paper from Patty and folding it. "I can sign it, even if I have to use my left hand. I'm going to give it to Mr. Martin for, some-how, I don't want to talk about the matter to him."

"I don't see why," said Patty, a little puzzled.

"Never mind, girlie. You know sometimes there are little foolish reasons we don't like to tell of. Don't say anything about all this to anybody, will you?"

"No, certainly not," said Patty, wonderingly.

"Don't tell any one I asked you to write the note."

"No."

"You see, I hate to acknowledge a hurt finger. It sounds so silly."

The whole affair seemed silly to Patty, for she could see no reason why Daisy shouldn't tell Guy that she didn't want to be Spirit of the Sea. But it was none of her affair, and as Daisy went away she put the whole matter out of her mind. After making a leisurely toilette, she went downstairs and found a group of young people having tea on the veranda. Her appearance was hailed with shouts of joy. Seats were offered her in every choice position, but the pleading look in Farnsworth's big blue eyes persuaded her to sit beside him in a broad, red-cushioned swing.

"You're all right, little girl, aren't you?" he said, anxiously, and Patty laughed gaily up at him as she answered, "Yes, indeed! and all ready for another adventure, if YOU'LL take care of me!"

"You apple blossom!" whispered Bill. "I won't hold you to your word, but I'd like to. Do you know, I've promised to be Father Neptune in this dinky parade they're getting up. Won't I be the gay old Sea Dog! I hope you'll be the Spirit of the Sea."

"That isn't decided; don't ask me about it yet," said Patty, who had no mind to commit herself until Guy should ask her definitely to take the part. Though since Lora couldn't take it, and Daisy wouldn't, she felt pretty sure it would fall to her.

A number of the Spring Beach boys and girls had drifted in, as they often did at tea time, and the talk of the many small groups was all of the coming festivity. Beside the Sea Float, there were the various rivers to be represented. The Nile would be characterised by Egyptian costumes and effects. The Hudson would be an attempt at a representation of "The Half Moon." The Tiber was to show gorgeous Roman citizens; the Thames proudly contemplated a houseboat, and the Seine, French scenery. Also, there would be floats representing Venice, Holland, the Panama Canal, Niagara Falls, the Open Polar Sea, and many others showing some phase or manifestation of water's great kingdom.

Daisy had inveigled Guy Martin into a tete-a-tete corner with her, but after a polite quarter of an hour, he declared he must move around and confer with a few people concerning their parts in the carnival.

"How about Patty's being Spirit of the Sea?" he asked.

"Oh," Daisy said, "you'd better not say anything to her about that. I asked her, and she gave me this note to give you. It isn't signed, nor addressed, but you see it's her handwriting. She wrote it hastily, but she said she didn't want to talk about the matter."

Guy looked a little surprised, but took the note and read it. "H'm," he said, "rather NOT be Spirit of the Sea. Get some one else. And - as a personal favour, don't speak of the matter to her! Well, Pretty Patty must have a miff of some sort. Most unlike her! However, her word is law. I'll never mention the subject to her, since she asks me not to. But our time is getting short, and most of the girls have their parts.

Miss Dow, won't you be Spirit of the Sea?"

"Why, yes, if you want me to," said Daisy, looking modest and demure. "I can make the costume easily, because I know just how. It requires fishnet draperies over green chiffon, and lots of seaweed decorations and that sort of thing."

"Yes; you have just the right idea. Then I'll put you down for that. You and Mr. Farnsworth will make a fine pair. I wonder what Patty WOULD like to be."

"I'll ask her," volunteered Daisy. "I know you're awfully busy, Mr. Martin, and I want to help you all I can. So leave that matter to me."

"Very well, I will," said Guy, who really had a multitude of cares and affairs; "but be sure to make her take some good part. It wouldn't be a Pageant at all with Patty Fairfield left out! If I didn't have to skip away this very minute to keep an engagement with a scene painter, I'd ask her what's the matter, anyhow!"

"Oh, Mr. Martin, you forget she asked you, as a personal favour, not to speak to her about it."

"By Jove! So she did! Wonder what's come over the girlie! If anybody has offended her, I'll kill him! Well, I must fly, Miss Dow; attend the rehearsals, won't you? See you tomorrow."

Guy made hasty adieux to Mona, and went off on his errands.

Daisy, in high spirits at the success of her ruse, went straight over to Patty.

"Patty, dear," she said, sweetly, "I couldn't withstand Mr. Martin's persuasions, and I've promised him I'll be the Spirit of the Sea. You know I told you I didn't want to, but he overruled my objections and I consented."

"All right, Daisy," said Patty, without a trace of regret on her sweet face. She did feel regret keenly, for Guy had asked her long ago, and she had only hesitated out of generosity toward Lora, who also wanted it. But it was not her nature to resent such things, and she concluded that Guy thought Daisy better adapted for the part than herself.

"What part will you take?" Daisy went on. "Mr. Martin told me to ask you and arrange for you."

Daisy's manner showed such undue importance and ostentatious authority that Jack Pennington spoke up.

"Are you assistant chairman, Miss Dow?"

"Mr. Martin didn't call it that," said Daisy, smiling pleasantly; "he only left it to me to see that Miss Fairfield had a good place in the Pageant."

"You bet Miss Fairfield will have a good place!" exclaimed Jack. "Don't you bother about it, Miss Dow. Let me relieve you of that duty. I'LL see to Miss Fairfield's place."

"But Mr. Martin left it in my care," persisted Daisy, getting a little frightened lest her deceit about the note should be discovered.

"Leave Mr. Martin to me," said Jack, a little curtly. "I'll explain to him that I relieved you of the responsibility of Patty's place in the show. I say, Patty, let's you and me be Dutch kiddies on the Holland Float."

"Shall us?" said Patty, smiling in a whimsical way that meant nothing at all.

CHAPTER XIV

PAGEANT PLANS

As Patty was preparing for bed that night, Mona came tapping at her door.

"Come in," said Patty. "Oh, it's you, Mona, - well, I AM glad to see you! In the turmoil of this 'house party' of yours, we almost never see each other alone, do we?"

"No; and I'm sorry. But you're enjoying it, aren't you, Patty?"

"Yes, indeed! I love it! People running in and out all the time, and a lot of people all over the house, - oh, yes, it's gay."

"Patty, I'm bothered about this Pageant business. How does it happen that Daisy has taken your part?"

"It wasn't my part. It had never been assigned, until Guy persuaded Daisy to take it."

"Persuaded fiddlesticks! She MADE him give it to her."

"No, she didn't. She was determined NOT to have that

part, but he coaxed her into it. She told me so herself."

"Pooh! You don't know Daisy as I do. You're so sweet and generous yourself you think everybody else is. I wish I hadn't asked her here. I thought she had outgrown her school-girl tricks. She was always like that."

"Like what?"

"Nothing; never mind. What does Bill say about it?"

"Nothing. I don't believe he knows who's to be Spirit of the Sea. And probably he doesn't care."

"Probably he DOES! Don't be a goose, Patty Fairfield! You know that great big angel Bill adores the ground you walk on."

"Is he as fond of Real Estate as all that? Well, I can't give it to him, for it's your ground that I'm on most of the time, and I suppose the beach is owned by the Realty Company or something."

"FUNNY girl! Patty, you make me laugh boisterously with that wit of yours! Well, Miss Sweetness, will you help me with my costume? Guy has 'persuaded' ME to be Cleopatra on the Nile Float."

"Oh, Mona, how lovely! You'll be a PERFECT Cleopatra. Indeed I will help you! What are you going to wear?"

"Whatever's the right thing. Of course it must be magnificent in effect. I'm going to send for a dress-maker and two helpers to-morrow morning, and put them to work on it. They can fit linings while I send to New York for the material. Lizette can go and select it. What do you think of gold-brocaded white satin?"

"Appropriate enough for Cleopatra, but ridiculous for a pantomime costume! Get white paper muslin or sateen, and trace a design on it with gold paint."

"No, sir-ee! I don't get a chance to shine as a dramatic star often, and I'm going to have the finest costume I can think up!"

"Oh, Mona, you have no sense of proportion," laughed Patty; "go ahead then, and get your white satin, if it will make you happy."

Apparently it would, and the two girls discussed the Cleopatra costume in all its details, until the little clock on the dressing-table held its two hands straight up in shocked surprise.

After Mona left her, Patty gave herself a scolding. It was a habit of hers, when bothered, to sit down in front of a mirror and "have it out with herself" as she expressed it.

"Patty Fairfield," she said to the disturbed looking reflection that confronted her, "you're a silly, childish old thing to feel disappointed because you weren't chosen to be Spirit of the Sea! And you're a mean-spirited, ill-tempered GOOSE to feel as you do, because Daisy Dow has that part. She'll be awfully pretty in it, and Guy Martin had a perfect right to choose her, and she had a perfect right to change her mind and say she'd take it, even if she HAD told you she didn't want it! Now, Miss, what have you to say for yourself? Nothing? I thought so. You're vain and conceited and silly, if you think that you'd be a better Spirit of the Sea than Daisy, and you show a very small and disagreeable nature when you take it so to heart. Now, WILL you brace up and forget it?"

And so practical and just was Patty's true nature that she smiled at herself, and agreed to her own remarks. Then dismissing the whole subject from her mind, she went to bed and to sleep.

Next day she went in search of Laurence Cromer, and found that young man sketching in a corner of one of the picturesque terraces of "Red Chimneys."

"Why these shyness?" asked Patty, as he quickly closed his sketch-book at her approach. "Why these modest coquetry? Art afraid of me? Gentle little me? Who wouldn't hurt a 'squito? Or am it that I be unworthy to look upon a masterpiece created by one of our risingest young artists?"

"I don't want you to see this sketch till it's finished," said Cromer, honestly. "It's going to be an awfully pretty bit, but unfinished, it looks like the dickens. Let me sketch you, Miss Fairfield, may I?"

"Yes, indeed; but can you talk at the same time? I want your advice."

"Oh, yes; the more I talk the better I work. Turn a little more to the right, please. Oh, that's perfect! Rest your fingertips on the balustrade, so - now, don't move!"

"Huh," remarked Patty, as Cromer began to sketch in swiftly, "how long do I have to stand this way? It isn't such an awful lot of fun."

"Oh, DON'T move! This is only a beginning, but I'll make a wonderful picture from it. That shining white linen frock is fine against the gleaming, sunlit marble of the terrace."

"All right, I'll stand," said Patty, goodnaturedly. "Now you can return the favour by helping me out of a quandary. Won't you advise me what part to take in the Pageant? As a matter of fact, I think all the best parts are assigned, and I don't want to be 'one of the populace,' or just 'a voice heard outside'! I want a picturesque part."

"I should say you did! Or, rather the picturesque parts all want you. Now, I'M designing the Niagara Float. It's unfinished, as yet, - the scheme, I mean, - but I know I want a figure for it, a sort of a, - well, a Maid of the Mist, don't you know. A spirituelle girl, draped all in grey misty tulle, and dull silver wings, - long, curving ones, and a star in her hair."

"Lovely!" cried Patty. "And do you think I could be it?"

"Well, I had a brown-haired girl in mind. Your colouring is more like 'Dawn' or 'Spring' or 'Sunshine.'"

"Oh, I HATE my tow-head!" exclaimed Patty. "I wish I was a nut-brown maid."

"Don't be foolish," said Cromer, in a matter-of-fact way. "You are the perfection of your own type. I never saw such true Romney colouring. Pardon me, Miss Fairfield, I'm really speaking of you quite impersonally. Don't be offended, will you?"

"No, indeed," said Patty. "I quite understand, Mr. Cromer. But what part AM I adapted for in the Pageant?"

"If you will, I'd like you to be Maid of the Mist. As I say, I had thought of a darker type, but with a floating veil of misty grey, and grey, diaphanous draperies, you would be very effective. Turn the least bit this way, please."

Patty obeyed directions, while she thought over his idea. "Maid of the Mist" sounded pretty, and the artist's float was sure to be a beautiful one.

"Yes, I'll take that part, if you want me to," she said, and Mr. Cromer said he would design her costume that afternoon.

"Hello, Apple Blossom!" called a big, round voice, and Bill Farnsworth came strolling along the terrace. Perched on his shoulder was Baby May, her tiny hands grasping his thick, wavy hair, and her tiny feet kicking, as she squealed in glee.

"Misser Bill my horsie," she announced. "Me go ridy-by."

"IS there something on my shoulder?" asked Bill, seemingly unconscious of his burden. "I thought a piece of thistledown lighted there, but it may have blown off."

"There is a bit of thistledown there," said Patty, "but don't brush it off. It's rather becoming to you."

"Indeed it is," agreed Cromer. "I'd like to sketch you and that mite of humanity together."

"You're ready to sketch anybody that comes along, seems to me," observed Bill. "Isn't this Miss Fairfield's turn?"

"I expect she's about tired of holding her pose," said the artist. "I'll give her a rest, and make a lightning sketch of you two. Baby's mother may like to have it."

"Oh, give it to me!" begged Patty. "I'd love to have a picture of Baby May."

"But there'll be so much more of me in it than Baby May," said Bill, gravely.

"Never mind," laughed Patty. "I shan't object to your presence there. Now, I'll run away while you pose, for I MIGHT make you laugh at the wrong time."

"Don't go," pleaded Bill, but Patty had already gone.

"What a beautiful thing she is," said Cromer, as he worked away at his sketch-block. He spoke quite as if referring to some inanimate object, for he looked at Patty only with an artist's eye.

"She is," agreed Bill. "She's all of that, and then some. She'll make a perfect Spirit of the Sea. I say, Cromer, help me rig up my Neptune togs, will you?"

"Of course I will, old chap. But Miss Fairfield isn't going to be on your float. She's agreed to be my Maid of the Mist."

"She HAS! I say, Cromer, that's too bad of you! How did you persuade her to change her plan?"

"She didn't change. She had no idea of being on your float. She asked me what I thought she'd better be, and she said all the most desirable parts were already assigned."

"H'm, quite so! Oh, of course, - certainly! Yes, yes, INDEED!"

"What's the matter with you, Bill? Are you raving? Your speech is a bit incoherent."

"Incoherent, is it? Lucky for you! If I were coherent, or said what I'm thinking, you'd be some surprised! You go on making your pencil marks while I think this thing out. All right, Baby; did Uncle Bill joggle you too much? There, - now you're comfy again, aren't you? I say, Laurence, I'll have my picture taken some other day. Excuse me now, won't you? I have a few small fish to fry. Come, Babykins, let's go find mummy."

"H'm," said Laurence Cromer to himself, as Bill swung off with mighty strides toward the house. "Somehow, I fancy he'll regain his lost Spirit of the Sea, or there'll be something doing!"

Baby May was gently, if somewhat unceremoniously, deposited in her mother's lap, and Bill said gaily, "Much obliged for this dance. Reserve me one for to-morrow morning at the same hour. And, I say, Mrs. Kenerley, could you put me on the trail of Miss Fairfield?"

"She went off in her runabout with Roger Farrington. I think she's heading for the telegraph office to order much materials and gewgaws for the Pageant."

"Then, do you know where Daisy Dow is? I MUST flirt with somebody!"

"Try me," said pretty little Mrs. Kenerley, demurely.

"I would, but I'm afraid Baby May would tell her father."

"That's so; she might. Well, Daisy is at the telephone in the library; I hear her talking."

"Thank you," said Big Bill, abruptly, and started for the library.

"Yes," he heard Daisy saying as he entered the room, "a long, light green veil, floating backward, held by a wreath of silver stars ... Certainly ... Oh, yes, I understand ... Good-bye."

She hung up the receiver, and turned to see Bill looking at her with a peculiar expression on his handsome, honest face.

"What are you going to represent in your light green veil, Daisy?" he asked.

"The Spirit of the Sea," she replied. "I've arranged for the loveliest costume, - all green and shimmery, and dripping with seaweed."

"How did you happen to be chosen for that part, Daisy?"

"Guy Martin insisted upon it. He said there was no one else just right for it."

"How about Patty Fairfield?"

"Oh, she WOULDN'T take it. She told Guy so."

"She did! I wonder WHY she wouldn't take it?"

"I don't know, Bill, I'm sure. It COULDN'T have been because you're Neptune, could it?"

"It might be," Bill flung out, between closed teeth, and turning, he strode quickly away.

"Bill," called Daisy, and he returned.

"What is it?" he said, and his face showed a hurt, pained look, rather than anger.

"Only this: Patty asked Guy as a special favour not to mention this matter to her. So I daresay you'll feel in honour bound not to speak of it."

"H'm; I don't know as my honour binds me very strongly in that direction."

"But it MUST, Bill!" and Daisy looked distinctly troubled. "I oughtn't to have told you, for Patty trusted me not to tell anybody."

"Patty ought to know better than to trust you at all!" and with this parting shaft, Bill walked away. On the veranda he met Guy Martin, who had called for a moment to discuss some Pageant plans with Mona. Guy was just leaving, and Bill walked by his side, down the path to the gate.

"Just a moment, Martin, please. As man to man, tell me if Patty Fairfield refused to take the part of the Spirit of the Sea?"

"Why, yes; she did," said Guy, looking perplexed. "It's a queer business and very unlike Patty. But she wrote me a note, saying she didn't want the part, and asking me not to mention the matter to her at all."

"She did? Thank you. Good-bye." And Bill returned to the house, apparently thinking deeply.

"Hello, Billy Boy, what's the matter?" called Mona, gaily, as he came up the veranda steps.

"I'm pining for you," returned Bill. "Do shed the light of your countenance on me for a few blissful moments. You're the most unattainable hostess I ever house-partied with!"

"All right, I'll walk down to the lower terrace and back with you. Now, tell me what's on your mind."

"How sympathetic you are, Mona. Well, I will tell you. I'm all broken up over this Pageant business. I wanted Patty Fairfield on the float with me, and she won't take the part, and now Daisy has cabbaged it."

"I know it. But Patty says Guy Martin chose Daisy in preference to her. And she says it's all right."

"Great jumping Anacondas! She says THAT, does she? And she says it's all right, does she? Well, it's just about as far from all right as the North Pole is from the

South Pole! Oh - ho! E - hee! Wow, wow! I perceive a small beam of light breaking in upon this black cat's pocket of a situation! Mona, will you excuse me while I go to raise large and elegant ructions among your lady friends?"

"Now, Bill, don't stir up a fuss. I know your wild Western way of giving people 'a piece of your mind,' but Spring Beach society doesn't approve of such methods. What's it all about, Bill? Tell me, and let's settle it quietly."

"Settle it quietly! When an injustice has been done that ought to be blazoned from East to West!"

"Yes, and make matters most uncomfortable for the victim of that injustice."

Big Bill calmed down. The anger faded from his face, his hands unclenched themselves, and he sat down on the terrace balustrade.

"You're right, Mona," he said, in a low, tense voice. "I'm nothing but an untamed cowboy! I have no refinement, no culture, no judgment. But I'll do as you say; I'll settle this thing QUIETLY."

As a matter of fact, Bill's quiet, stern face and firm-set jaw betokened an even more strenuous "settlement" than his blustering mood had done; but he dropped the whole subject, and began to talk to Mona, interestedly, about her own part in the Pageant.

CHAPTER XV

IN THE ARBOUR

After returning from her motor ride with Roger, Patty went to her room to write some letters.

But she had written only so far as "My dearest Nan," when a big pink rose came flying through the open window and fell right on the paper.

Patty looked up, laughing, for she knew it was Bill who threw the blossom.

The bay window of Patty's boudoir opened on a particularly pleasant corner of the upper veranda, - a corner provided with wicker seats and tables, and screened by awnings from the midday sun. And when Patty was seated by her desk in that same bay window, half-hidden by the thin, fluttering curtain draperies, Big Bill Farnsworth had an incurable habit of strolling by. But he did not respond to Patty's laughter in kind.

"Come out here," he said, and his tone was not peremptory, but beseechingly in earnest. Wondering a little, Patty rose and stepped over the low sill to the veranda. Bill took her two little hands in his own two big ones, and looked her straight in the eyes.

"What part are YOU going to take in this foolish racket they're getting up?" he asked.

"I'm going to be Maid of the Mist," answered Patty, trying to speak as if she didn't care.

"Why aren't you going to be Spirit of the Sea?"

"Because Guy asked Daisy to take that part."

"Yes! he asked her after you had refused to take it!"

"Refused! What do you mean?"

"Oh, I know all about it! You wrote a note to Martin, telling him you wouldn't take the part, and asking him not to mention the subject to you again."

"What!" and all the colour went out of Patty's face as the thought flashed across her mind what this meant. She saw at once that Daisy had given that note to Guy, as coming from HER! She saw that Daisy MUST have done this intentionally! And this knowledge of a deed so despicable, so IMPOSSIBLE, from Patty's standpoint, stunned her like a blow.

But she quickly recovered herself. Patty's mind always JUMPED from one thought to another, and she knew, instantly, that however contemptible Daisy's act had been, she could not and would not disclose it.

"Oh, that note," she said, striving to speak carelessly.

"Yes, THAT NOTE," repeated Bill, still gazing straight at her. "Tell me about it."

"There's nothing to tell," said Patty, her voice trembling a little at this true statement of fact.

"You wrote it?"

"Yes, - I wrote it," Patty declared, for she could not tell the circumstance of her writing it.

Bill let go her hands, and a vanquished look came into his eyes.

"I - I hoped you didn't," he said, simply; "but as you did, then I know WHY you did it. Because you didn't want to be on the float with me."

"Oh, no,-NO, Bill!" cried Patty, shocked at this added injustice. "It wasn't THAT, - truly it wasn't!"

Gladness lighted up Bill's face, and his big blue eyes beamed again.

"Wasn't it?" he said. "Wasn't it, Apple Blossom? Then, tell me, why DID you write it?"

"But I don't want to tell you," and Patty pouted one of her very prettiest pouts.

"But you shall tell me! If you don't," - Bill came a step nearer, - "I'll pick you up and toss you up into the top branches of that biggest pine tree over there!"

"Pooh! Who's afraid?"

Patty's saucy smile was too much for Bill, and, catching her up, he cradled her in his strong arms, and swung her back and forth, as if preparatory to pitching her into the tree.

"Here you go!" he said, laughing at her surprised face. "One, - two -"

"Mr. Farnsworth!" exclaimed a shocked voice, and Aunt Adelaide came hastening toward them.

Bill set Patty down, not hastily, but very deliberately, and then said, with an anxious air:

"How did it go, Mrs. Parsons? We're practising for our great scene in the Pageant - the Spirit of the Sea, tossed by old Father Neptune. I do my part all right, but Miss Fairfield needs more practice, don't you think so?"

Aunt Adelaide looked scrutinisingly at the young man, but his expression was so earnest that she couldn't doubt him.

"Patty looked scared to death," she said, with reminiscent criticism. "Oughtn't she to look more gay and careless?"

"She certainly ought," assented Bill. "Will you try the scene once more, Miss Fairfield, with Mrs. Parsons for audience?"

"I will not!" exclaimed Patty, and trying hard to repress her giggles, she fled back through her window, and drew the curtains.

"I didn't know you were to have acting on the floats," said Aunt Adelaide, innocently.

"I'm not sure that we shall," returned Farnsworth,

easily. "I had a notion it would be effective, but perhaps not. Do you know where Miss Dow is, by any chance?"

"Why, I think she's just starting for the Sayres'. Yes, there she goes now, - walking down the path." "WILL you excuse me then, Mrs. Parsons, if I make a hurried exit? I want to see her on a MOST important matter."

Big Bill fairly flung himself down the little staircase that led from the upper veranda to the lower one, and in a few moments, with long strides, he had overtaken Daisy, who was alone.

"Whoop-ee! Daisy, wait a minute!" he cried, as he neared her.

"What for?" and Daisy turned, smiling, but her smile faded as she caught sight of Bill's face.

"Because I tell you to!" thundered Bill. "Because I want to talk to you, - and, right now!"

"I - I'm going on an errand -" faltered Daisy, fairly frightened at his vehemence.

"I don't care if you're going on an errand for the Czar of Russia; you turn around, and walk along with me."

"Where to?"

"Wherever I lead you! Here's a rose arbour, this will do. In with you!"

Daisy entered the arbour, trembling. She had never seen Farnsworth so angry before, and her guilty conscience made her feel sure he had discovered her treachery. In the arbour they were screened from observation, and Bill lowered his voice.

"Now," said he, "tell me all about this 'Spirit of the Sea' business. What underhanded game did you play to get the part away from Patty Fairfield?"

"I didn't! She told Guy Martin she wouldn't take it."

"Yes; she wrote him a note. Now, in some way or other, you made her write that note. How did you do it?"

"Did she tell you I made her write it?"

"No, she didn't! She said she wrote it, but she wouldn't tell me why."

Daisy's eyes opened wide. Then Patty KNEW the note had been given to Guy in her name, and yet she didn't denounce Daisy! Such generosity was almost outside Daisy's comprehension, and she paused to think it out. At last she said:

"Why do YOU think she wouldn't tell you?"

"I don't THINK, I KNOW! A man has only to look into Patty Fairfield's clear, honest eyes to know that she's incapable of meanness or deceit. While you, - forgive me, Daisy, but I've known you for years, - and you ARE capable of gaining your own ends by under-handed methods."

"What do you accuse me of?" and Daisy's air of injured innocence was well assumed.

"I don't know," and Bill looked exceedingly perplexed. "But I DO know that in some way you persuaded Patty to give up that part, because you wanted it yourself."

Daisy drew a long breath of relief. Then, she thought, he didn't know, after all, just what she HAD done, and perhaps she could carry it through yet.

"You're mistaken," she said, in a kind way, "Patty did write that note, but she had her own reasons, and she desired, especially, that no one should mention the subject to her."

"Yes," said Bill, "and it's that strange reluctance to having the subject mentioned that makes me suspect YOUR hand in the matter. Patty refused to discuss it with me, but the look of blank astonishment in her face, when I referred to that note, convinced me there's a bit of deviltry SOMEWHERE. And I ascribe it to you!"

"You do me an injustice," and now Daisy's tone was haughty and distant; "but I cannot resent it. For Patty's sake, I too must refuse to discuss this matter. Think of me as you will, - I cannot defend myself."

Daisy's face grew so sad and martyr-like that generous-hearted Bill was almost convinced of her innocence.

"I say, Daisy," he began, "if I'm wronging you in this matter, I'll never forgive myself."

"Oh, never mind, Bill; I'm used to being misunderstood. But I'll forgive you, if you'll promise never to refer to the subject again to me, or to any one else."

Bill might have promised this, but the too eager gleam in Daisy's eyes again roused his suspicions. And just then he saw Patty crossing a bit of lawn near them.

"Whoo-ee!" he called, and as Patty turned, he beckoned for her to come to them.

"What's wanted?" called Patty, gaily, as she neared the arbour.

"You," said Bill, while Daisy sank down on the arbour seat, and seemed to crumple up in abject fear of what was about to happen.

"Now, Miss Fairfield," Bill began, "there's a little matter I want cleared up. It's the note you wrote to Mr. Martin saying you didn't wish to be Spirit of the Sea."

Daisy cast one piteous, despairing glance at Patty, and then covered her face in her hands.

At first, Patty's blue eyes flashed with a righteous indignation, to think how Daisy had abused her kindness in writing that note at dictation. Then a great wave of compassion swept through her heart. The deed was so foreign to her own nature that she felt deep pity for one who was capable of such a thing. And Daisy's evident misery roused her sympathy. She didn't stop to think that probably Daisy's regret was at being found out and not for the deed itself, but Patty's forgiveness was full and free, even before it was asked. In her unbounded generosity of heart, she resolved to shield Daisy from Farnsworth's wrath.

"What about the note?" she asked, simply.

"Did you write it?"

"I did."

"Did any one force or persuade you to write it?"

"I did it willingly, and without compulsion."

"Did Daisy know you wrote it?"

"She knew it, yes. She gave it to Guy Martin."

Bill was nonplussed. He KNEW there was some secret about that note, but he couldn't quite fathom it.

And every word Patty spoke, though quite true, and seeming to exonerate Daisy, made the guilty girl more and more amazed that one she had so injured COULD be so forgiving.

"Didn't you want to be Spirit of the Sea?" Bill said at last, desperately anxious on that point.

Patty hesitated. She couldn't truly say she didn't, and to say she did would bring up the question of the note again.

"I DID want to," she said, slowly, "but, since Daisy has that part, - and I have another, and a very pretty part, - I am quite content."

"Then there is nothing more to be said," Farnsworth muttered. "The incident is closed."

He started to leave the arbour, and Daisy lifted her troubled eyes to Patty's face. Patty tried to smile, but there must have been an involuntary shadow of reproach in her blue eyes, which, for some reason, went straight to Daisy's heart.

"DON'T look at me like that, Patty," she cried out; "I can't bear it! Bill, come back! The incident ISN'T closed. I want to tell you, Bill, what I did. Patty wrote that note, at my dictation, thinking it was for me, - I had a hurt finger, - and I told her I'd sign it, - and I DIDN'T sign it, - I gave it to Guy as if it was from her - oh, Patty - will you forgive me? WILL you?"

"There, there, Daisy," and Patty put her arms around the sobbing girl. "Never mind, it's all right."

"It isn't all right!" exclaimed Farnsworth, his eyes blazing. "Daisy Dow, do you mean to tell me -"

"She doesn't mean to tell YOU anything," interrupted Patty. "She's only going to tell me. I wish you'd go away. This note matter is entirely between Daisy and myself. It's - it's a sort of a - a joke, you see."

Daisy sat up straight, and stared at Patty. What sort of a girl was this, anyhow, who could forgive so freely and fully, and then call it all a JOKE!

But Daisy knew generosity when she saw it, and with her heart overflowing with gratitude at Patty's kindness, she bravely acknowledged her own fault.

"It ISN'T a joke, Bill," she said, in an unsteady voice. "I did a horrid, hateful thing, and Patty is so angelic and forgiving she makes me feel too mean to live."

"Nonsense," said Patty, "there's no harm done, I'm glad

you owned up, Daisy, for now we can forget the whole episode, and start fresh."

But Farnsworth couldn't toss the matter aside so easily.

"Daisy," he said, looking at her sternly, "I never heard of such a mean piece of business in my life! I think -"

"Never mind what you think!" cried Patty, turning on him like a little fury. "YOU'RE the MEAN one, - to rub it in when Daisy is feeling so bad over it."

"She ought to feel bad," growled Bill.

"Well, she DOES, if that's such a comfort to you," retorted Patty. "Now, go away, and leave us girls alone, won't you? This is our own little sewing circle, and we don't want any men at it."

Patty was really so relieved at the turn things had taken, that she gave Bill a happy smile, which contradicted her crusty words.

"No, I won't go away," he declared; "you girls want to weep on each other's shoulders, - that's what you want. I'm going to stay and see the performance."

"You can't stay, unless you'll say you forgive Daisy, and love her just the same."

"Just the same as who?" demanded Bill, quickly, and Patty blushed adorably.

"Just the same as you always did," she returned, severely.

"Do forgive me, Bill," said Daisy, contritely; "I'm awfully sorry."

Farnsworth looked at her, squarely. "I'll forgive you, Daisy," he said, "if you'll make good. Let Patty take the Spirit of the Sea part, and you take something else."

"I won't do it," said Patty, quickly, but Daisy said, "Yes, you must. I shan't feel that you've really forgiven me unless you do."

As a matter of fact, Daisy saw little prospect of pleasure for herself in being Spirit of the Sea, after all this, and she doubted whether Bill would be Neptune if she did.

Patty demurred further, but both the others coaxed so hard that she finally yielded to their persuasions.

"What will the others say?" she asked, at last.

"Nothing at all," responded Bill, promptly. "Simply announce that you and Daisy have agreed to change parts. Then Daisy can be 'Maid of the Mist,' and you can be the Water Sprite of old Neptune's float."

"I'll do it, on one condition," said Patty; "and that is, that no one else is let into our secret. Let Guy continue to think that I sent him that note, but that I changed my mind about it. And don't tell anybody at all, not even Mona, the truth of the matter."

"Gee! You're a wonder!" exclaimed Farnsworth, and Daisy threw her arms round Patty's neck and kissed her.

"Oh, don't give me undue credit," Patty said, laughing; "but, you see, I just naturally hate a 'fuss,' and I want to forget all about this affair right away. Daisy, you're just the sort of brown hair and eyes Mr. Cromer wants for his Maid of the Mist. You'll be perfectly sweet in that."

"You're perfectly sweet in everything, Patty; I never saw any one like you!"

"Neither did I," said Farnsworth, with emphasis.

"Oh, here you are," drawled a slow voice, and Laurence Cromer came sauntering along in search of Patty. "Don't you want to discuss your costume now? There's only a half-hour before luncheon time."

"Well, you see, Mr. Cromer," said Patty, smiling at him, "you said you wanted a more brownish lady for your misty maid. So Miss Dow and I have decided to change places."

"All right," agreed Cromer. "It makes no difference to me, personally, of course. I'm merely designing the Niagara Float as an architect would. I think perhaps a brunette would be better adapted to the part of Maid of the Mist, as I have planned it, but it's as you choose."

"Then we choose this way," declared Patty.

"Run along, Daisy, and Mr. Cromer will tell you just what to get for your misty robes."

Daisy went away, and Farnsworth turned to Patty with a reproachful glance.

"You let her off too easy," he said. "A girl who would do a thing like that ought to be punished."

"Punished, how?" said Patty, quietly.

"Her deceit ought to be exposed before the others. It oughtn't to be hushed up, - it makes it too easy for her."

"Her deceit, as you call it, affected no one but me. Therefore, there's no reason for any one else to know of it. And Daisy has been punished quite enough. I read in her eyes the sorrow and remorse she has suffered for what she did. And I know she did it on a sudden impulse, - an uncontrollable desire to have that particular part in the Pageant. Now, I have forgiven and forgotten it all, it's but a trifle. And I can see no reason why YOU should still hold it against her."

Farnsworth looked steadily into Patty's eyes, and a sort of shamed flush rose to his cheeks.

"You're bigger than I am, Little Girl," he said, as he held out his hand.

Patty put her little hand into his, and in that understanding clasp, they buried the subject never to refer to it again.

"Oh, no, I'm not really bigger than you," she said, lightly.

"Not physically, no," he returned, looking down at her. "If you were, I couldn't toss you into a treetop!"

"You got out of that beautifully with Aunt Adelaide," and Patty laughed at the recollection. "But I'm going to scold you for picking me up in that unceremonious fashion."

"I know, - it WAS dreadful! But, - perhaps I did it on a sudden impulse, - you know, - you forgive THOSE!"

Patty remembered her defence of Daisy, and couldn't repress a smile at the boy's wheedlesome argument.

"Well, don't let it happen again," she said with an attempt at extreme hauteur.

But Farnsworth replied, "When I get a real good chance, I'm going to pick you up and carry you a million miles away."

"Catch me first!" cried Patty, and darting away from him, she ran like a deer toward the house.

Farnsworth stood looking after her, but made no move to follow.

The big fellow was thinking to himself, wondering and pondering in his slow, honest way, on why that little scrap of pink and white humanity had all unconsciously twined herself around his very heartstrings.

"Apple Blossom!" he murmured, beneath his breath, and then sauntered slowly toward the house.

CHAPTER XVI

THE SPIRIT OF THE SEA

The night of the Pageant was as beautiful as the most exacting young person could desire. There was no moon, but there seemed to be an extra bright scattering of stars to make up for it. A soft, cool ocean breeze stirred the air, there was no dampness, and everybody pronounced the evening as perfect as if specially made for the occasion.

An early dinner was served at "Red Chimneys," and then the guests dispersed to don their carnival costumes.

With her usual promptness, Patty was ready first, and coming down to the drawing-room, found nobody there. So she took opportunity to admire her own effects in the multitude of mirrors.

It was an exquisite reflection that faced her. She had not adopted Daisy's idea of fishnet, as that seemed to her too heavy. Laurence Cromer had approved of her own suggestions, and together they had designed her costume. It was of pale green chiffon, trailing away in long, wavy lines. Over it, hung from the shoulders a tunic-like drapery of white chiffon. This was frosted, here and there, with broken, shimmering lines of silver, and the whole effect hinted of moonlight on the sea.

Patty's wonderful hair fell in curling, tumbling masses over her shoulders and far down her back. In it were twined a few strands of seaweed, - beautifully coloured French work, which Laurence Cromer had procured from somewhere by a very special order. Across the top of her head a silver band confined the riotous curls, and from it, in the centre, rose an upright silver star.

Though simple, the whole costume was harmonious and picturesque, and suited Patty's fair beauty to perfection. Her bare arms and throat were soft and rounded as a baby's, and her lovely face had a pink glow of happiness, while her eyes were like two starlit violets.

She peacocked about the room, frankly delighted at her own reflection in the mirrors, and practised the pose she was to assume on the Float.

In the mirror she saw that a majestic figure was entering the room, and wheeling swiftly about, she beheld Father Neptune himself smiling at her.

Farnsworth had sent to a theatrical costumer in the city for his garb, and very handsome he looked in a dark green velvet robe that hung in classic folds. He wore a snow-white wig and long white beard, and a gold and jewelled crown that was dazzlingly regal. He carried a trident, and in all respects, looked the part as Neptune is so often pictured. Patty gazed at him a moment in silent admiration, and then sprang to her pose, lightly poised forward, her weight on one foot, and her arms gracefully outspread.

Big Bill held his breath. Always lithe and graceful, to-night Patty looked like a veritable spirit. Her floating draperies, her golden hair, and her perfect face, crowned with the single silver star, seemed to belong to some super-human being, not to a mere mortal.

Big Bill walked slowly toward her.

"Patty!" he murmured, almost beneath his breath. "Apple Blossom! I want you so!"

A lovelier pink rose to Patty's cheeks, for it was impossible to mistake the earnestness in Bill's voice. She smiled at him, gently for a moment, and then roguishly, and her dimples flashed into view, as she danced lightly away from him, calling back over her shoulder, "Catch me first!"

"You'll say that once too often yet, my lady!" declared Farnsworth, as he stood with folded arms looking after her, but not following her dancing footsteps.

At the hall doorway, Patty turned and looked back, down the long room. Farnsworth stood where she had left him, and his majestic pose, as he held his gilded trident, suited well his stalwart, magnificent physique.

"Come back here," he said, and his voice was not dictatorial, but quietly compelling.

Slowly Patty danced down the room, swaying, as if in rhythm with unheard music. As she came to a pause in front of Farnsworth, she made him a sweeping, mocking courtesy.

"Father Neptune, god of the Sea!" she said, as if

offering homage.

Farnsworth raised his hand, dramatically.

"Spirit of the Sea," he said, "Nymph of the silver-crested waves, kneel before me!"

Catching his mood, Patty sank gracefully on one knee, bowing her fair head before the majestic sea-god.

"I crown thee," Neptune went on, "fairest of all nymphs, loveliest of all goddesses. Spirit of the Sea, but also, maiden of the apple blossoms."

Patty felt a light touch on her bowed head, but did not move, until a moment later, Neptune held out his hand.

"Rise, Spirit of the Sea, crowned by Neptune, god of the Ocean!"

Patty rose, and in a nearby mirror saw her crown. It was a slender wreath of wonderfully fine workmanship. Leaves of fairy-like silver filigree, and tiny apple blossoms, of pink and white enamel. Light in weight, soft, yet sparkling in effect, it rested on her fair head, in no way interfering with the silver star that flashed above it. Indeed, it seemed the last touch needed to perfect the beauty of Patty's costume, and her face was more than ever like an apple blossom as she turned to thank Farnsworth for his gift.

But before she could do so, several people sprang in from the hall, where they had been watching the coronation ceremony.

"Hooray for you two!" cried Roger. "You show true

dramatic genius! Patty, you're a peach to-night! Bill, you're a hummer!"

Only Daisy was unsmiling. A pang of jealousy thrilled her heart, as she saw the exquisite picture Patty made, and saw, too, the lovely gift Farnsworth had given her. Daisy's costume was beautiful and exceedingly artistic, but the grey, misty garb seemed tame beside Patty's clear coloured draperies and bright, sea-weed tangled hair.

"Patty, you're wonderful!" Mona exclaimed. "If I weren't so weighted down with this dragging train, I'd hug you!"

Mona looked regal in her Cleopatra costume. She had chosen a rich white and gold brocaded satin, and the gold lace on the train which hung from her shoulders, made it heavy indeed. She was loaded with jewels, both real and paste, and her Egyptian headdress was both gorgeous and becoming. Mona had never looked so well, and Roger, who was Father Nile, expressed his admiration frankly.

"I say, Mona," he declared, "if the real Cleo Pat looked like you, I don't blame old Mark for flirting with her. Maybe I'll flirt with you before the evening is over."

"Ha! Minion! Methinks thou art presumptuous!" said Mona, marching about theatrically. But she smiled at Roger, for the two had become good friends.

Adele and Jim Kenerley were Dutch young people, and in blue and white cotton costumes, looked as if they had just alighted from an old Delft platter.

Laurence Cromer took no costume part, as he had to direct the posing of the characters and the scenic details of the parade.

Mrs. Parsons was enchanted with the gorgeousness of her party of young people, and when Patty gave her a sprig of seaweed to tuck in her bodice, she felt as if she belonged to the water carnival.

Motors carried the laughing crowd to the Sayres' house, from where the floats were to start.

Of course Old Ocean's Float led the parade. Though not very realistic, it was a theatrical representation of the sea, and the great billows, made of green muslin crested with cotton batting and stretched over somewhat wabbly framework, tossed and swayed almost like the Atlantic breakers. At the back end of the float was a great canopied throne, on which sat the gold-crowned Neptune holding his firmly planted trident. Before him seemed to dance the Spirit of the Sea, for Patty, now in one pose and now in another, was outlined against the dark billows with charming effect. A bright electric light streaming from a point above the throne, illuminated both characters and threw into relief the shells and seaweed that decorated the sides of the float.

The other floats were equally well done, - some even better in artistic conception. Each received uproarious applause as it rolled slowly along the line of march. Hotels and cottages were all illuminated, and the whole population of Spring Beach was out admiring the Pageant.

"Aren't you tired, Patty?" asked Farnsworth, gently, as

she changed her pose.

"Yes, I am," she confessed; "but it isn't the posing, - it's the jolting. I had no idea the ocean was so rickety!"

"Poor little girlie! I wish I could do something for you. But we have to go a couple of miles further yet. Can you stand it!"

"Yes; but I'd rather SIT it!"

"Do! Come and sit on this throne beside me. There's plenty of room."

"Oh, nonsense, I couldn't. What would the people think?"

"Do you want to KNOW what they'd think?" returned Farnsworth, promptly. "They'd think that you were old Neptune's Queen, and that you meant to sit beside him all the rest of your life. Let them think that, Patty, - and, let it be true! Will you, my apple blossom girl?"

"No, Bill," said Patty, quietly, and changed her pose so that she did not face him. His words had startled her. Above the rumbling of the float, she had heard him clearly, though, of course, they could not be overheard by the laughing, chattering bystanders.

His earnest tones had left no room for doubt of his meaning, and after Patty's first shock of surprise, she felt a deep regret that he should have spoken thus. But in an instant her quick wit told her that she must not think about it now. She must turn a laughing, careless face to the passing audience.

"Nay, nay, Neptune," she said, facing him again, "I must play my own part. If a life on the ocean wave is not as easy as I had hoped, yet must I brave it out to the end."

Farnsworth took his cue. He knew he ought not to have spoken so seriously at this time, but it was really involuntary. He had fallen deeply in love with the Eastern girl, and his Western whole-heartedness made it difficult for him to conceal his feelings. He flashed a warm, sunny smile at her and said heartily:

"All right, Sea Sprite! I know your pluck and perseverance. You'll get there, with bells on! Take the easiest pose you can, and hang on to that foam-crested wave near you. It sways a bit, but it's firmly anchored. I looked out for that, before I trusted you to this ramshackle old hay wagon!"

Patty smiled back, really helped by his hearty sympathy and strong, ringing voice.

"I HATE to be so, - so unable to stand things!" she exclaimed, pouting a little.

"You're no Sandow girl," he replied; "but - one can't expect an apple blossom to be as strong as a - a cabbage!"

"Nor as strong as a great big Westerner," she returned, looking admiringly at the stalwart Neptune, and thereby pleasing him greatly, for Big Bill was honestly proud of his pounds and inches.

At last they reached the Country Club, which was their destination, and the parade was over; though as the carnival was to conclude with a supper and a dance for the participators, the best part of the fun was yet to come. Aunt Adelaide, who had reached the clubhouse a little earlier, was waiting for her charges, and Bill promptly escorted Patty to her.

"Look after this little girl, won't you, Mrs. Parsons?" he said. "She'll be O. K. after a few moments' rest, but a seafaring life is a hard one, and this little craft is glad to get into port."

Patty gave him a grateful glance, and said:

"Nonsense, Aunt Adelaide, I'm not really tired, but I just want to sit down a while. My feet have a headache!"

"I don't wonder!" declared Mona. "It was awful for you to perch on one toe for a hundred million mile ride! And I reclined at ease on a Roman trident, or whatever you call it!" "Tripod, you mean," said Adele, laughing, "or is it trireme?"

"Dunno," said Mona, who was arranging Patty in a soft easy-chair in the dressing-room of the club. "Now, you sit there, you Sea Witch," she commanded, "and I'll have a maid bring you a hot bouillon or a weak tea, whichever you prefer. You can't have coffee, it might spoil that pinky-winky complexion of yours."

"Nothing can spoil that!" said Daisy, and though the remark sounded complimentary, it was prompted by a spirit of jealousy. Daisy had truly appreciated Patty's generosity in the matter of the note but she couldn't gracefully submit to having her own brunette beauty eclipsed by what she called a doll-face.

Patty's weariness was purely muscular, and so of short duration, and after ten minutes' rest, she was feeling as fresh as ever.

"Now, what do we do?" she asked, shaking her draperies into place and adjusting the new wreath on her hair.

"Now comes the supper," said Mona, "and I'm glad of it. Come on, girls."

The long dining hall at the club was a pretty sight. The guests were all in their Pageant costumes, and as the various float groups mingled, the contrasts were effective. A Venetian gondolier escorted a fisher girl of the Seine, or a bold buccaneer from the Spanish Main clanked his sword in time with the clatter of the wooden sabots of a Holland lass.

Neptune was waiting to escort the Spirit of the Sea to a table, but as Patty came through the dressing-room door, Captain Sayre bowed before her, and asked the honour of taking her to supper. As Farnsworth had made no engagement with Patty, merely taking it for granted that she would go with him, she saw no reason to decline Captain Sayre's invitation, and went gaily away with him.

Farnsworth gazed after her with a look of dazed bewilderment.

"Had you asked her?" said an amused voice, and turning, he saw Mrs. Parsons at his elbow.

"No! I was too stupid to think of it!"

"Patty is so very popular, you know, it's difficult to secure her favours. Have you engaged any dances?"

"No! What an idiot I am! You see, Mrs. Parsons, I'm not really a 'society man,' and in these formal affairs, I'm a bit out of my element. Will you do me the honour to go to supper with me?"

Aunt Adelaide looked at the towering figure in its regal velvet robes.

"I oughtn't to," she said, with a little laugh, "but I can't resist the temptation. So I will! The idea of MY going with the king of the whole show!"

"Excepting Miss Fairfield, there's no one I'd rather have," said Big Bill, honestly, and so Father Neptune strode majestically to his seat at the head of the table, and at his right sat primly, fluttering Aunt Adelaide, instead of the witching sprite he had expected to place there.

Patty was really glad, for she didn't wish to appear too exclusively with Farnsworth, and yet she was a little disappointed, too, for as the Spirit of the Sea, her place was by Father Neptune.

But Captain Sayre made himself very entertaining, and as Jack Pennington was on her other side, she soon forgot all about Little Billee, and gave herself up to the fun of the moment.

"I well remember your beautiful dancing," said the captain. "Will you give me some waltzes?"

"I don't give them plurally," said Patty, smiling at him.

"I'll give you one, perhaps; a half one, anyway."

"Not enough!" said Captain Sayre, decidedly. "I must have more than that, by fair means - or otherwise. Where is your card?"

"I haven't any yet; won't it be time enough to get one after supper?"

"Yes, if you let me see it before any one else. I find it's a trick with the young men here to make dance engagements surreptitiously at the supper table."

Patty glanced about, and saw more than one tasselled card appearing and disappearing from hand to hand.

A moment later, she heard a voice behind her chair. "Apple Blossom," it whispered, "I've brought you a dance card. Say 'Thank you, Bill.'"

"Thank you, Father Neptune," said Patty, flashing a smile at him, as she took the card, and turned back to the captain.

CHAPTER XVII

THE APPLE BLOSSOM DANCE

"Now I have a programme, Captain Sayre," Patty said. "If you really want a part of a dance -"

"I don't!" declared the captain, positively. "There are some ladies I'd dance half a dance with, but NOT with you."

"Then I suppose I'll have to give you a whole one," Patty sighed, "and I know I won't have enough to go 'round. You know it's late, and there are only ten dances on the list."

"And they're half gone!" exclaimed Captain Sayre, as he looked at the card Patty had handed him.

"What!" she cried, looking at it herself.

Sure enough there was a very big black B. F. written against every other dance!

"Bill Farnsworth!" she exclaimed. "Well, if he hasn't a nerve! He wants the earth!"

"And the sea, and all that in them is!" said Captain Sayre. "Look here, Miss Fairfield, I'll be satisfied with the other five. Thus, you're dividing your dances evenly, don't you see?"

"Nonsense! I'll agree to no such highway robbery! You may have a dance, Captain Sayre, - take a waltz, if you like; and then give me my card again. Do you want one, Jack?"

"DO I? Does a squirrel want nuts? Only one, Sea Spirit?"

"Yes, only one. It's such a short programme to-night."

"And is Big Bill to have five?"

"Indeed, no! I shall cross those all off but one."

Learning, somehow, of what was going on, most of the men at the table began to beg Patty for a dance, and in a few moments her card was filled.

She shook her head reprovingly at Farnsworth, who quite understood the reason.

Supper over, the dancing began, and as it was a summer evening, the dances alternated with cooling strolls on the long verandas of the club house. Patty loved to dance, and greatly preferred good dancers for partners.

Captain Sayre was especially proficient in the art, and as their dance was followed by an "extra," he persuaded Patty to do a fancy dance with him, like they had danced at the Sayres' garden party. Soon most of the dancers had paused to watch the two, swaying and pirouetting in a dance, partly impromptu, and partly fashioned on some they had previously learned. It was a pretty sight. Patty, whose step was light as thistledown, followed any hint of Captain Sayre's, and so clever were his leads that the audience broke into loud applause. It was almost more than Farnsworth could bear. He stood looking at them with such a wistful expression that Patty concluded to stop.

"I'm a little tired," she whispered to her partner, "but I want to dance a moment alone. Will you let me? And ask the orchestra to play the Spring Song."

"I'll love to look at you," declared the captain, and at the end of a measure, he gracefully danced away from her, and Patty stood alone.

The rest had all ceased dancing now, preferring to watch, and as they were nearly all Patty's friends and acquaintances, she felt no embarrassment.

"The Apple Blossom Dance," she said, and flung herself into a series of wonderful rhythmic motions that seemed to give hint of all the charms of spring. One could almost see flowers and hear birds as the light draperies swayed like veils in a soft breeze. And then, with a fleeting glance and smile at Farnsworth, Patty plucked apple blossoms from overhanging boughs, and tossed them to the audience. There were no trees, and there were no blossoms, but so exquisite was her portrayal of blossom time, and so lovely her swaying arms and tossing hair that many were ready to declare they could even detect the fragrance of the flowers. But when Patty essayed to stop, the riotous applause that followed and the cries of "Encore! encore!" persuaded her to dance once more, though very tired.

More languidly this time the apple blossoms were plucked from the branches, more slowly the springtime steps were taken, and before she reached a point in the music where she could stop, Patty was swaying from faintness, not by design.

Farnsworth saw this, and acting on a sudden impulse, he swung the great folds of his trailing velvet over his arm, and with a few gliding steps, reached her side, threw an arm round her, and suiting his steps to hers, continued the figure she had begun. But he supported her weary little form, he held her in a strong, firm clasp, and, a fine dancer himself, he completed the "Apple Blossom Dance" with her, which she never could have done alone. Then, after bowing together to the delighted and tumultuously applauding audience, he led her to a seat, and shielded her from the unthinking crowd, who begged her to dance for them again.

"Little Billee, you're a dear!" said Patty, as the next dance took the people away again. "How did you know I was going to sink through the floor in just one more minute?"

"I saw how tired you were, and though I hated to 'butt in' on your performance, I just felt I had to, to save you from collapse."

"You DIDN'T 'butt in'! You're a beautiful dancer, better than Captain Sayre, in some ways, though you don't know so many fancy steps. But you picked up my idea of the apple blossom steps at once!"

"Because that's OUR dance. And you're my property to-night, anyway. Didn't Neptune crown the Spirit of the Sea?"

"Yes, and I haven't yet thanked you for this lovely wreath! It's the most beautiful thing! Where DID you get it?"

"I had it made, to replace the one I stole from you the night of the storm."

"You didn't steal that, - I gave it to you."

"Well, and so I give you this one in return. Will you wear it sometimes?"

"I'll wear it often, it's so lovely. And SO becoming, - isn't it?"

Naughty Patty smiled most provokingly up into the big blue eyes that looked intently at her.

"Becoming?" he said. "Yes, it IS! What isn't becoming to you, you little beauty?"

"There, there, don't flatter me!" and Patty cast down her eyes demurely. "Oh, Jack, is this our dance?" And with a saucy bow, Patty left Big Bill, and strolled away on Jack Pennington's arm.

"You're a regular out and out belle to-night, Patty," he said, frankly. "All the men are crazy over you, and all the girls are envious."

"'Tisn't me," said Patty, meekly. "It's this ridiculous green rig and my unkempt hair."

"Shouldn't wonder," returned Jack, teasingly; "girls always look best in fancy dress."

"So do the boys," Patty retorted. "Isn't Bill Farnsworth stunning in that Neptune toga, - or whatever it's called?"

"Pooh, you'd think he was stunning in anything, wouldn't you?"

"Oh, - I don't know -' and Patty put her fingertip in her mouth, and looked so exaggeratedly shy that Jack burst into laughter.

"You're a rogue, Patty," he declared. "If you don't look out you'll grow up a flirt."

"Am I flirting with you?" and Patty opened her eyes very wide in mock horror at such an idea.

"No, - not exactly. But you may, if you like."

"I DON'T like!" said Patty, decidedly. "We're good chums, Jack, and I want to stay so. No flirt nonsense about us, is there?"

"No," said Jack; "let's dance," and away they whirled in a gay two-step.

When the dancing was over, the "Red Chimneys" party started for home in various motors. Patty thought Bill would ask her to ride with him, but he didn't come near her, and she wondered if he were annoyed or offended in any way.

She confessed to feeling a little tired, and rode quietly beside Aunt Adelaide, leaning her sunny head on that lady's shoulder.

"But it was lovely!" she said, with a sort of purr like a contented kitten. "I'd like to have a Pageant every night!"

"Yes, you would!" exclaimed Roger, who sat in front of her in the big motor. "You'd be dancing in a sanitarium next thing you knew."

"Pooh!" retorted Patty. "I'm not a decrepit old invalid yet, am I, Aunt Adelaide?"

"No, dearie; but you must take care of yourself. I think a cold compress on your forehead to-night would do you good."

"And a hot compress on my chin, and two lukewarm ones on my ears," teased Patty, laughing at the solicitous tones of the older lady. "No, sir-ee! I'll catch a nap or two, and tomorrow I'll be as right as a - as a - what's that thing that's so awfully right?"

"A trivet," said Mona.

"Yes, a trivet. I've no idea what it is, but I'll be one!"

There was a light supper set out in the dining-room at "Red Chimneys," but no one wanted any, so good-nights were said almost immediately and the wearied revellers sought their rooms.

"No kimono parties to-night, girls," said Patty, firmly. "I'm going straight to bed."

"All right," agreed Mona and Daisy, "we'll save our gossip till morning."

Carolyn Wells

But Patty didn't go straight to bed. She flashed on the lights in her rose-coloured boudoir, drew the curtains of the bay window, and then threw herself into a big easy-chair. She was thinking of Mr. William Farnsworth. She wished he hadn't said what he had. It worried her, somehow. And when he said good-night just now, he had a look in his eyes that meant, - well, perhaps it didn't mean anything after all. Perhaps he was only flirting, - as Patty herself was. But was she? She had just asked herself this question, really seriously, when a rose came flying in at the window and fell at her feet. She looked up quickly, - she was SURE she had drawn the curtains. Yes, she had done so, but there was just a little space between them, where they didn't quite join.

Well, it must have been a good marksman who could throw so accurately! Westerners were accounted good marksmen, - it MIGHT be-

And then a second rose followed the first, and others, at intervals, until a good-sized heap lay at Patty's feet.

Laughing in spite of herself, she went to the window, and peeped out between the curtains.

"Why, it's you!" she exclaimed, as if she hadn't known it all the time.

"Yes," and Big Bill smiled at her over the armful of roses he still held. "I've completely stripped the rose garden, but I had to bombard you with something!"

"Are you a bombardier?"

"No, I'm a beggar. I'm begging you to come out here

for a few minutes and see the moonlight on the ocean."

"Why, there isn't any moon!"

"That's so! I mean the sun."

"Well, the sun isn't QUITE up yet!"

"That's so! Well, I mean the - the stars, - there, I knew SOMETHING was shining!"

Bill's laugh was so infectious that Patty couldn't help joining it, but she said:

"I can't, Little Billee. It's too late, and I'm too tired, and -"

"But I'm going away to-morrow."

"You are! I didn't know."

"Do you CARE? Oh, Patty, come out for a minute, I want to tell you something."

Still in her green draperies and silver wreath, Patty stepped out on the veranda, saying, "Just for a tiny minute, then."

Bill had discarded his Neptune trappings, and in evening dress, was his handsome self again.

"You were fine as Neptune," said Patty, looking at him critically as he stood against a veranda pillar, "but you're better as a plain man."

"Thank you!" said Bill, ironically.

"Fishing! Well, I DIDN'T mean that you're plain, but, - I won't say what I did mean."

"Oh, dear! Another fond hope shattered! I WISH I knew what you DID mean!"

"Don't be silly, or I'll run back. If you'll promise not to be silly, I'll stay another minute."

"But, you see, I never know when I am silly."

"Almost always! Now let's talk about the Pageant. Didn't Daisy look pretty?"

"Yes. But I fancy blondes myself."

"Now that's ambiguous. I don't know whether you mean because you're one or because I'm one."

"Why! So you ARE a blonde, aren't you? I never noticed it before!"

"Really? How nice! I've always wondered how I'd strike an entire stranger!"

"Why strike him at all?"

"Now you're silly again! But I mean, I'd like to know what an utter stranger would think of me."

"I hate to be called an utter stranger, but I haven't the least objection to saying what I think of you. In fact, I'd like to! May I?'

"Is it nice?" asked Patty, frightened a little at Bill's quiet tones.

"Judge for yourself. I think you are the most beautiful girl I have ever seen, - and the most fascinating. I think you have the sweetest nature and disposition imaginable. I think you have just enough perversity to give you the Zip you need."

"What is Zip?"

"Never mind; don't interrupt. I think you are the most adorable fluff of femininity in the world, - and I KNOW I love you, and I want you for all my very own. Patty, - DARLING, - tell me now what you think of ME."

"Oh, Bill, DON'T say such things to me, - PLEASE, don't!" And Patty's overstrung nerves gave way, and she began to cry.

"I won't, dear, - I won't, if it bothers you," and Big Bill's arm went round her in such a comforting way that Patty wept on his broad shoulder.

"Don't, - don't think me a silly," she said, smiling up at him through her tears, "but - I'm so tired, and sleepy, - if you could just wait till morning, - I'd tell you then what I think of you."

"Very well, dear, I'll wait."

"No, you needn't, I'll tell you now," and Patty suddenly drew away from Bill's arm and faced him bravely. "I'm a coward, - that's what I am! And I cried because, - because I can't say what you want me to, and - and I HATE to hurt your feelings, - because I LIKE you so much."

"Patty! do you KNOW what you're talking about?"

"Yes, I do! But I can't seem to say it out plain, without hurting your nice, big, kind heart."

"Let me say it for you, little girl. Is it this? Is it that you like me as a friend, and a comrade - chum, but you don't love me as I love you, and you're afraid it will hurt me to know it?"

"Yes, yes, that's it! How did you know?"

"You told me yourself, unconsciously. Now, listen, my girl. I only love you MORE for being brave and honest about it. And I love you more still for your dear, kind heart that can't bear to hurt anybody. And to prove that love, I'm not going to say any more to you on this subject, - at least, not now. Forget what I have said; let us go back to our good comradeship. I startled you; I spoke too soon, I know. So forget it, my apple blossom, and remember only that Little Billee is your friend, who would do anything in the world for you."

"You're an awfully nice man," said Patty, not coyly, but sincerely, as she laid her hand on his arm a moment.

"Now you HAVE told me what you think of me!" cried Farnsworth, gaily, and taking the little hand he held it lightly clasped in his own. "And I thank you, lady, for those kind words! Now, you can look at the moon just a minute longer, and then you must fly, little bird, to your nest in the tree."

"Yes, I must go. Tell me, Little Billee, where did you learn to dance so well?"

"It's mostly my natural grace! I took a few lessons of a wandering minstrel, out home, but I don't know the technique of it, as you and that ornamental captain do."

"But you could learn easily. Shall I teach you?"

"No, - Apple Blossom, I think not."

"Oh, there won't be time. You said you're leaving to-morrow! Must you go?"

"It doesn't matter whether I must or not. If you look at me like that, I WON'T! There, there, Sea Witch, run away, or - or I'll flirt with you!"

"Yes, it's time I went," said Patty, demurely, gathering up her draperies. "But, Billee, how can I thank you for the dear, sweet lovely wreath?"

"Well, there are several ways in which you COULD thank me, - though I'm not sure you WOULD. Suppose we just consider me thanked?"

"That doesn't seem much. Shall I write you a note?"

"That doesn't seem VERY much. Why don't you give me a gift in return?"

"I will! What do you want? A penknife?"

"Mercy, no! I'll have to think it over. Wait! I have it! Have your picture taken - with the wreath on, and give me that."

"All right, I will. Or perhaps Mr. Cromer would sketch me in this whole rig."

"PERHAPS he WOULD!" and Farnsworth caught his breath, as he looked at the vision of loveliness before him. "But we'll see about that later. Skip to bed now, Apple Blossom, and don't appear below decks before noon to-morrow."

"No, I won't. I'm awful tired. Good-night, Little Billee."

"Good-night, Apple Blossom Girl," and Farnsworth held aside the curtain as Patty stepped through the window.

A shower of flowers flew after her, for Bill had picked up his remaining posies, and Patty laughed softly, as the curtain fell and she stood in her room, surrounded by a scattered heap of roses.

"Just like a theatrical lady," she said, smiling and bowing to an imaginary audience, for Patty loved to "make-believe."

And then she took off her silver wreath and put it carefully away.

"Little Billee is SUCH a nice boy," she said, reflectively, as she closed the box.

CHAPTER XVIII

A COQUETTISH COOK

"Hello, Pattypet," said Mona, appearing at Patty's bedside next morning. "How's your chocolate? Does it suit you?"

"Delicious," said Patty, who was luxuriously nestling among her pillows while she ate her breakfast.

"Well, make the most of it, for you'll never get anything more fit to eat or drink in this happy home."

"What DO you mean?"

"Listen to my tale of woe. The chef and his wife have both left."

"Francois? And Marie! Why, whatever for?"

"Your English is a bit damaged, but I'll tell you. You see, Aunt Adelaide flew into one of her biggest tantrums, because her shirred egg was shirred too full, or her waffles didn't waff, - or something, - and she sent for Francois and gave him such a large piece of her mind that he picked up his Marie and walked off."

"Have they really GONE?"

"They really have. I've telephoned to the Intelligence Place, and I can't get a first-class cook down here at all. I shall have to send to the city for one, but, meantime - what to do! What to do!"

"H'm, - and you've guests for luncheon!"

"Yes, the whole Sayre tribe. The captain just CAN'T keep away from YOU! Patty, do you know you're a real belle? Everybody was crazy about you last night."

"Fiddlesticks! Just because I had on a green frock and let my hair hang down."

"Your hair is WONDERFUL. But I didn't come up here to tell you of your own attractions! I want your able advice on how to have a luncheon party without a cook."

"Oh, pooh! that's TOO easy! Give me a helper of some sort, and I'll cook your old luncheon. And I'll promise you it will be just grand!"

"Cook! You? I won't let you. What do you take me for? No, you come with me, and we'll go somewhere where cooks grow and BUY one."

"There won't be time, Mona. What time is luncheon to be?"

"Half-past one; and it's about ten now."

"Oceans of time, then; I tell you, I'll see to the kitchen for luncheon. But of course, you must have a cook, for permanent use."

"Well, rather. But I'll get one from New York by to-morrow morning. And you know Adele Kenerley's friends are coming to dinner to-night. What about that?"

"Leave all to me. I will arrange. But I want somebody to help me. How about Daisy?"

"Daisy's no good at that sort of thing. And I don't like to ask Adele. Say, Patty, let Bill help you; he's a fine cook, I've been on camp picnics with him, and I know. And maybe he wouldn't be GLAD to help you in anything! Ah, there, Patty, you're blushing! I feared as much! Oh, Patty, DO you like him?"

"'Course I like him. He's a jolly chap, and we're good chums."

"But is that all? Patty, tell me; I won't tell."

"There's nothing to tell, Mona. I like Little Billee a whole lot, but I'm not in love with him, if that's what you mean."

"Yes, that's what I mean. I hoped you were."

"Well, I'm not. And I'm not going to be in love with anybody for years and years. I'm fancy-free, and I mean to stay so. So don't try to tease me, for you won't get any fun out of it."

"That's so; you're too straightforward to be teased successfully. Patty, you've been a real lesson to me this summer. I've learned a lot from you. I don't mean to gush, but I DO want to tell you how I appreciate and cherish all the kindness you've shown me."

"Dear old Mona, I'm glad if I've said or done anything to make you feel like that! You're a trump, girl, and I'm glad to have you for a friend. Now, vanish, my lady, and as soon as I can scrabble into a costume, I'll meet you below stairs, and solve all your kitchen problems for you."

"But, Patty, I CAN'T let you go into the kitchen!"

"You can't keep me out, you mean! I'm delighted to have the chance. Aprons are terribly becoming to me."

"Do you want one of the parlourmaid's aprons?"

"I do not! I want a big, all-enveloping cook's apron."

"Well, I suppose you don't want a man's. I'll find you one of Marie's."

"I don't care whose it is, if it's big. Skip, now!"

Mona vanished, and Patty jumped out of bed, and dressed for her new work. She chose a pink-sprigged dimity, simply made, with short sleeves and collarless neck. A dainty breakfast cap surmounted her coil of curls, donned, it must be confessed, because of its extreme becomingness. Mona provided a large, plain white apron, and going to the kitchen, Patty considered the situation.

The viands for the luncheon had arrived, but were not in the least prepared for use. A large basket showed a quantity of live crabs, which lay quietly enough, but a twitching claw here and there betrayed their activity.

"Mercy!" cried Mona, "let's throw these away! You

can't do anything with these creatures!"

"Nonsense," said Patty, "I'm versed in the ways of crabs. I'll attend to them. What else, Mona?"

"Oh, here are some queer looking things from the butcher's. I don't know what they are. Can they be brains?"

"No, they're sweetbreads, and fine ones, too. And here is the romaine for the salad, and lovely squabs to roast. Oh, Mona, I'm just in my element! I LOVE to do these things; you know I'm a born cook. But I must have a helper."

"I know; Marie always helped Francois. They were a splendid pair. It's a pity Aunt Adelaide had to stir them up so, - and all over nothing."

"Well, don't cry over spilt eggs. I'll do up this luncheon, and I'll fix it so I can slip up and dress, and appear at the table as if nothing had happened. The waitress and the butler can manage the serving process?"

"Oh, yes. I HATE to have you do it, Patty, but I don't know what else to do. Here, I'll help you."

Patty had already filled a huge kettle with boiling water, and was about to put the crabs in it.

"All right, Mona; catch that side of the basket, and slide them in, all together. It seems awful to scald them, but the sooner the quicker. Now, - in they go!"

But in they DIDN'T go! One frisky crab shot out a

Carolyn Wells

long claw and nearly grabbed Mona's finger, which so scared her that she dropped her side of the flat basket, and the crabs all slid out on the floor instead of into the kettle.

With suddenly aroused agility they scuttled in every direction, some waggling to cover under tables and chairs, and some dancing about in the middle of the floor.

Hearing Mona's shrieks and Patty's laughter, Daisy came running down. But the sight was too horrifying for her, and she turned and sped back upstairs. Poor Daisy was not so much to be blamed, for having lived all her life in Chicago, she had never chanced to see live crabs before, and the strange creatures were a bit startling.

She flew out on the veranda and caught Big Bill by one sleeve, and Roger by another.

"Come! Come!" she cried. "Patty and Mona are nearly killed! Oh, hurry! You'll be too late!"

"Where, where?" cried Roger, while Farnsworth turned white with the sudden shock of Daisy's words. He thought some dreadful accident had happened, and fear for Patty's welfare nearly paralysed him.

"This way! That way!" screamed Daisy, darting toward the kitchen stairway, and then flying back again.

Down the stairs raced the two men, and into the kitchen. There they found Patty standing on a side table, armed with a long poker, while Mona danced about on the large table, brandishing a broom in one hand and a mop in the other. Patty was in paroxysms of laughter at Mona's antics, but Mona herself was in terror of her life, and yelled like a wild Indian.

"Get down! Go 'way!" she cried, as an adventurous crab tried, most ineffectually, to climb the table leg.

Roger sprang on to the table beside Mona. "There, there," he said, "you rest a while, and I'll holler for you. Go 'way! Get down! Go 'way, you!"

His imitation of Mona's frightened voice was so funny Patty began to laugh afresh, and Farnsworth joined her.

"Get up here on my table, Little Billee," cried Patty. "You'll be captured and swallowed alive by these monsters!"

Big Bill sat on the corner of Patty's table and looked at her.

"You make a charming little housewife," he said, glancing at the cap and apron.

"Help me, won't you?" Patty returned, blushing a little, but ignoring his words. "I'm going to cook the luncheon, and first of all we must boil these crabs. Can't you corral them and invite them into that kettle of water? We had them started in the right direction, but somehow they got away."

"Right-o!" agreed Bill, and placing the toe of his big shoe gently on a passing crab, he picked it up by the hinge of its left hind leg, and deftly dropped it in the boiling water.

"That's just the right way!" said Patty, nodding approval. "I can pick them up that way, too, but there are so many sprinkled around this floor, I'm afraid they'll pick me up first."

"Yes, they might, Apple Blossom. You sit tight, till I round them all up. Lend a hand, Farrington."

So Roger poked out the unwilling creatures from their lairs, and Bill assisted them to their destination, while the two girls looked on.

"Good work!" cried Patty as the last shelly specimen disappeared beneath the bubbles. "Now, they must boil for twenty minutes. They don't mind it NOW."

The girls came down from their tables, and explained the situation.

"Don't worry, Mona," said Farnsworth, in his kind way. "Patty and I will cook luncheon, and this afternoon I'll go out and get you a cook if I have to kidnap one."

"All right, Bill," said Mona, laughing. "Come on, Roger, let's leave these two. You know too many cooks spoil the broth!"

"So they do!" called Bill, gaily, as Mona, after this parting shaft, fled upstairs. "Do I understand, little Apple Blossom," he observed, gently, "that you're really going to cook this elaborate luncheon all yourself?"

"Yes, sir," said Patty, looking very meek and demure.

"CAN you do it?"

"Yes, sir." Patty dropped her eyes, and drew her toe along a crack in the floor, like a bashful child.

"You little rascal! I believe you can! Well, then, you can be chef and I'll be assistant. I WAS going to arrange it the other way."

"Oh, no, sir! I'll give the orders." And Patty looked as wise and dignified as a small bluebird on a twig.

"You bet you will, my lady! Now, first and foremost, shall I pare the potatoes?"

"Oh, Billee, there must be a scullery maid or something for that!"

"Don't see any, and don't want any! I'm not afraid of staining my lily-white fingers. You'd better put those sweetbreads in cold water to blanch them, and cut up some bread to dry out a little for the squab stuffing."

"For goodness gracious sake! Do you know it all?" exclaimed Patty, looking at him in amazement.

"Yes, I know everything in all the world. I'm a terrible knower!"

"You are so! How did you learn it all?"

"Born so. Are you going to have that sort of a grape fruit muddle in glasses?"

"Yes; with candied cherries in it. Don't you love it?"

"Yes, if you do. What thou lovest, I will love, and thy discards shall be mine also."

"Amiable boy! Now, don't talk to me, I have to measure these things very carefully."

"Oh, I say! Let me make the salad dressing. I'm a hummer at it, and I don't measure a thing."

Patty looked at him coldly.

"If you turn out to be a BETTER cook than I am," she said, "I'll never speak to you again!"

"Oh, I'm not! I'm a FEARFUL cook! I spoil everything I touch! DON'T ask me to make that dressing! DON'T!"

Patty couldn't help laughing at his foolishness, and the work went merrily on.

But picking out the crabs was a tedious task. It was easy enough, and Patty was deft and dainty, but it took a long time, and the sharp shells cut her fingers now and then.

"Let me do it, dear," said Farnsworth, quietly, and he took from her the fork she was using.

"Oh, thank you!" she said, gratefully. "You ARE a help, Little Billee."

"I'm always ready to help YOU, Patty girl; call on me any time, anywhere; if ever you want me, - I'm right there."

"I think somebody else might have helped us with these crabs, anyway."

"They would, if we asked them. I like it better this way. Alone with thee, - just you and me, - the crabs to free, - is bliss for we!"

"Speak for yourself, John! I don't see any bliss in picking out crabs. I've cut and scratched every single solitary finger I possess!"

"Poor little girl! But, you see, I offer you my hand, - both hands, in fact, - there's ten extra fingers at your disposal, if you want them. And all willing and eager to work for you."

"Mr. Farnsworth, how do you suppose I can make croquettes if you talk to me like that? One table-spoonful of flour, - two of butter, three eggs -"

"Pooh, can't you read a recipe and be proposed to at the same time?"

"Yes, I CAN," Patty flashed back, "but, - I pay attention only to the recipe!"

"'Twas ever thus," Bill sighed.

"What! EVERY time you've proposed?" said Patty, roguishly.

"No, because I've never proposed before. Don't you think I do it well for a beginner?"

"Not very."

"Not very! You little scamp, what do you know about it? Have you had a wide experience in proposals?"

"I shouldn't tell you if I had. One of flour, two of butter, three -"

"Three blithering wheelbarrows! Apple Blossom, have you any idea how I love you?"

"Don't put me out, Bill. One of flour, two of butter, three eggs -"

"Now, isn't she the limit?" mused Bill, apparently addressing the crabs. 'I express my devotion in terms of endearment, and she babbles like a parrot of flour and butter!"

"If I don't, you'll have no croquettes," and Patty moulded the mixture into oval balls, and arranged them in a frying sieve.

As the time grew shorter they worked away in earnest, and soon after one o'clock everything was ready. The finishing touches and the serving of the hot dishes were left to the butler and waitress, who were none too willing to do anything outside their own restricted sphere, but whom Patty cajoled by smiles, till they were her abject slaves.

"Now go and tidy yourself up," Patty said to Bill, "and I will too, and see who can get down to the drawing-room first."

"Huh, I haven't to arrange a lot of furbelows. I'll beat you all to pieces."

But he little knew Patty's powers of haste in emergency, and when fifteen minutes later he descended to the drawing-room, where the guests were already arriving, Patty was there before him.

She was in a soft, frilly white frock, with knots of pale blue ribbon here and there, the knots holding sprays of tiny pink rosebuds. A blue ribbon banded her head, and save for an extra moist curliness in the soft rings of hair on her temples, no one could have guessed that the serene looking girl had worked hard and steadily for three hours in a kitchen.

"I surrender," whispered Bill; "you're the swiftest little piece of property I ever saw!"

"Please address me in less undignified language," said Patty, slowly waving a feather fan.

Bill bent a trifle lower, and murmured close to her ear, "Mademoiselle Apple Blossom, you are the sweetest thing in the world."

CHAPTER XIX

A FORCED MARCH

After luncheon they all strolled out on the verandas or through the gardens, and Patty and Mona slipped away to hold a council of war by themselves.

"You're a darling, Patty," Mona said, "and I was perfectly amazed at those wonderful messes you fixed up for luncheon."

"I don't approve of the term you apply to my confections!"

"Well, you know what I mean. They were all PERFECT, you fairly outdid Francois."

"That's better. Now, Mona mine, we must acquire some servants, and that right speedily."

"Yes, but how? I think I'd better telephone the dinner guests not to come."

"I'd hate to do that. They're Adele's friends, and she's so anxious to have them come here."

"I know it, but what can we do? I won't let you cook again."

"No, I don't want to cook dinner. Luncheon seems different, somehow. But I do believe if I take Camilla, and scour all the plains around Spring Beach, I can catch something that can cook."

"I'd hate to have a poor cook."

"Yes, I know; I mean a first-class cook, though, perhaps not a chef."

"Well, go ahead, Patty, but you'll have to start at once. Your cook ought to be here by four, and it's almost three now."

"'I slip, I slide, I gleam, I glance,' - what comes next? Never mind, I'll just scoot."

Throwing on a white pongee dust cloak over her pretty frock, Patty declared herself ready to start, and Mona ordered an electric runabout brought from the garage.

But Miss Patricia Fairfield had no intention of going alone upon her quest. Walking up to a group of men talking on the veranda, she paused in front of Farnsworth.

"I want you," she said, calmly.

"I am yours," he responded with equal calm, and throwing away his cigar, turned to go with her.

"Don't you want me?" asked Captain Sayre, eagerly.

"And me?" added Cromer.

"I know you want me," put in Roger, "but you're too

shy to say so."

"I want you all," said Patty, beaming on the group, "but I like you one at a time, and this is Little Billee's turn."

"What's up, my lady?" said Farnsworth, as he started the swift little car.

"Why, just this. Turn toward the main road, please. We've simply got to find a cook for Mona within an hour. I KNOW we can do it, - but, YOU tell ME how."

"Dead easy, child. We'll just go out and kidnap one."

"But cooks aren't found sitting in deserted baby carriages, to be tempted with candy. Now be sensible. Can't you think of any plan?"

"Not a plan! Can you?"

"Well, all I can think of is to go to see Susan."

"Susan it is! Where does the lady reside?"

"Down this way two blocks, then turn to the right."

"She is won! We are gone! Over bank,
  bush and scar,
  They'll have fleet steeds that follow!" quoth
  young Lochinvar.'"

"I know Susan wouldn't come, but she may know of some one else," went on Patty. "Here we are; stop at this house."

"No, Miss Patty," said Susan, when the case was laid

before her, "I don't rightly know of anny wan for the place. I'd go mesilf, - for I'm a good, fair cook, - but I can't be afther makin' them fiddly-faddly contraptions Miss Galbraith has."

"Well, Susan, if we can find a cook, will you come as helper? Just for a few days, till Miss Galbraith can get some people down from New York."

"Yes, Miss Patty; I'll do that. Now, I'm bethinkin' me, there's the Cartwrights' cook. She's a perfessional, and the family has gone away for three days, sure. Cuddent she do ye?"

"Fine!" cried Patty. "Where do the Cartwrights live?"

"Up the road a piece, an' thin down beyant a couple o' miles. Don't ye know the big grey stone house, wid towers?"

"Oh, yes; I know where you mean. And is the cook there? What's her name?"

"Yes, she's there. An' her name is O'Brien. It's Irish she is, but she knows more cookin' than manny Frinch jumpin'-jacks! If she'll go wid yez, I'll go."

"Well, I'll tell you, Susan. You go on over to Miss Galbraith's now. Tell her I sent you, and that I'll bring Mrs. O'Brien in about half an hour. Then you go to the kitchen and get things started."

"My, it's the foine head ye have on ye, Miss Patty! That's a grand plan!"

Susan turned back to her sister's house, and the

motor-car darted forward.

"So far, so good," said Patty. "But now to get the O'Brien. Suppose she won't come?"

"Don't borrow trouble, Apple Blossom. Let's suppose she WILL come, and meanwhile let's enjoy our ride. It was dear of you to ask me to come with you."

"Well, you see, I didn't know but it might require force to persuade a cook to go back with us, and, - and you're so big, you know."

"Then I'm glad I'm so big, since brawn and strength win favour in my lady's sight."

"You ARE strong, aren't you?" and Patty looked at the giant beside her. "I think," she went on slowly, "your strength must be as the strength of ten."

"I hope so," and Farnsworth's voice took or a graver note, "and for the right reason."

Just then they came in sight of the Cartwright place.

"Good gracious!" cried Patty, as they drove in. "Here are four thousand dogs coming to meet us!"

Patty's estimate of their number was extravagant, but there WERE five or six dogs, and they were large and full-lunged specimens of their kind.

"I'm frightened," said Patty. "They're watchdogs, you know, turned loose because the people are away. Don't get out, Billee, they'll bit you! They're bloodhounds, I'm sure!"

"Then I'll play I'm Eliza crossing the ice, and you can sit here and be Little Eva."

Patty had to laugh at his foolishness, but the dogs WERE fierce, and she was glad when at last his repeated rings at the doorbell were answered.

"Nobody at home," said a voice, as the door opened only a narrow crack, and but part of a face could be seen.

"Is that so?" said Bill, pleasantly. "But you're at home, aren't you? And perhaps you're the very one I want to see. Are you Mrs. O'Brien?"

"Yes, I am," and the door opened just a trifle wider; "but the family is away, an' me ordhers is to admit nobody at all, at all."

"Well, we don't want to be admitted, but won't you step outside a moment?"

Farnsworth emphasised his remarks by pushing the door wide open, and, partly out of curiosity, Mrs. O'Brien stepped outside. She was a small woman, but her face wore a look of grim determination, as if she were afraid of nothing. She quieted the barking dogs, and turned to Patty.

"Don't be afraid, Miss," she said; "they won't hurt ye, now that they see me a-talkin' to yez. Did ye want to see Mrs. Cartwright? She ain't home, an' won't be till day after tomorrah."

"No," said Patty, "I don't know Mrs. Cartwright. I want to see you. Susan Hastings, my own cook, said your people were away, and so perhaps you would go out to cook for a couple of days to oblige a neighbour."

"Oblige a neighbour, is it? Sure no lady would come afther another lady's cook, underhanded like, when the lady's away!"

Patty's face flushed with righteous indignation.

"It ISN'T underhanded!" she exclaimed, "You don't understand! I don't want you PERMANENTLY, but only for a day, or two days at most, - because our cook has left."

"Arrah, ma'am, you said your cook was Susan Hastings! Yer a quare leddy, I'm thinkin', an' yer husband here, is another! Sthrivin' to entice away a cook as is satisfied wid her place, and who manes honest by her employers!"

Farnsworth was grinning broadly at the assumption of his and Patty's relationship, but Patty was enraged at the implication of underhandedness.

"He ISN'T my husband!" she cried, "and I don't want a cook for myself, but for another lady!"

"Are ye runnin' an intilligence office, belike?"

"Here!" cried Bill, sharply. "Don't you speak like that to that lady! Now, you listen to me. We are both visitors at Miss Galbraith's. Her cook left suddenly, and we want you to come and cook for us, two days if you will, - but one day ANYWAY! See? Do you understand that? You're to go over to Miss Galbraith's now, with us, and cook dinner tonight. After dinner, you may do as you like about staying longer. We'll pay you well, and there's no reason whatever why you shouldn't oblige us."

At first the Irishwoman looked a little intimidated at Bill's manner and his gruff tones, but in a moment she flared up.

"I'll do nothin' of the sort! I'm left here in charge of this place, an' here I'll shtay!"

"Is there no one else to guard the place?"

"Yis, there's the second gardener, an' the coachman. I cooks their meals for them. The other servants is away for two days."

"Well, the second coachman and third gardener, or whatever their numbers are, can cook for themselves to-night. You're going with us, - see? With US, - NOW!"

"I'll not go, sor -" began Mrs. O'Brien, but Big Bill picked the little woman up in his arms, as if she had been a child.

"This is a case of kidnapping a cook, Patty," he said. "I told you I'd do it!"

Paying no attention to his struggling burden, Farnsworth pulled shut the door of the Cartwrights' house, shook it to make sure it closed with a snap lock, and then gently but firmly carried Mrs. O'Brien to the motor-car.

"Take the driving seat, Patty," he directed, and, as she

did so, he deposited the cook in the seat beside her. Then he climbed into the small seat at the rear and remarked:

"Let her go, Patty; and unless you sit still and behave yourself, Mrs. O'Brien, you'll fall out and get damaged. Now be a nice cook, and make the best of this. You're kidnapped, you see, - you can't help yourself, - and so, what are you going to do about it?"

The cook sat bolt upright, her hard, unsmiling face looking straight ahead, and she replied, between clenched teeth, "Wanst I get out, I'll go straight back home, if it's a hundherd miles yez do be takin' me!"

"Oh, don't do that," and Patty's voice was sweet and coaxing. "Let me tell you something, Mrs. O'Brien. You know Susan Hastings, - what a nice woman she is. Well, once I was in a great emergency, worse even than to-day, and knowing the warm, kind hearts of the Irish, I went to Susan and asked her to help me out. And she did, - splendidly! Now, I know you've got that same warm Irish heart, but for some reason you don't WANT to help me out of my trouble. Won't you tell me WHAT that reason is?"

Mrs. O'Brien turned and looked at her.

"Me heart's warrum enough," she said, "an' I'd be glad to sarve the likes of such a pretty leddy as yersilf, - but, I won't shtand bein' carried off by kidnappers!"

"But listen," said Patty, who was beginning to hope she could cajole the woman into a good humour; "you must realise that the gentleman is a Western man. Now they do things very differently out there from what men do here. If they want anything or anybody they just TAKE them!"

"H'm, h'm," murmured Farnsworth, affirmatively over Patty's shoulder.

She paid no attention to his interruption, and went on, "So, you see, Mrs. O'Brien, you mustn't mind the rude and untutored manners of the savage tribes. This gentleman is a - is an INDIAN!"

"You don't tell me, Miss!"

"Yes, he is. And though you're perfectly safe if you do just as he tells you, if you rebel, he might - he might TOMAHAWK you!"

"Lor', Miss, is he as bad as that?"

"Oh, he's AWFUL bad! He's terrible! He's - why, he's IRRESISTIBLE!"

Big Bill was shaking with laughter, but Mrs. O'Brien couldn't see him, and Patty herself looked half scared out of her wits.

"Now, I'll tell you what, Mrs. O'Brien," she went on, "you let me be your friend; trust to me, and I'll see that no harm comes to you. If you'll cook this dinner to-night, I'll promise to send you home safely to-morrow morning, and Miss Galbraith will pay you well beside. Susan Hastings will be with you as a helper, and - and if you only make your mind up to it, you can have a real good time!"

Patty felt that she ended her speech rather lamely, but

her eloquence had given out. And the sound of Bill's chuckles, behind her, made it difficult not to laugh herself.

But either Patty's friendliness or fear of Bill's ferocity seemed to conquer Mrs. O'Brien's rebellious spirit, and she sat calmly in her place, though making no further observations.

Nor could Farnsworth and Patty converse, for as Bill sat behind, and they were flying rapidly along, speech was inconvenient if not impossible.

Farnsworth kept a sharp eye on his captive; though he knew she could not escape now, he wasn't sure what strange turn her temper might take. But Patty felt sure that if she could once get the cook into the kitchen at "Red Chimneys," and under the influence of Susan's common sense and powers of persuasion, all would be well. She drove round to the kitchen entrance, and as she stopped the car, Farnsworth jumped down to assist their passenger out.

Uncertain just how to show her unwillingness to do their bidding, Mrs. O'Brien sat still and refused to move. Whereupon, Patty jumped down and ran into the kitchen.

"Susan," she cried, "here's the cook! Come out and make her behave herself!"

Susan followed Patty out, and saw the new arrival.

"Is it yersilf, Ann O'Brien?" she cried, joyfully. "Come on in, now."

"I'll not come! These vilyans kidnapped me, and I'll cook no dinner fer the likes o' thim!"

"Arrah now, it's yersilf is the vilyan! Ye ought to be proud to be kidnapped by Miss Patty, and Misther Bill! Get down here, ye gossoon, an' behave like a dacint woman!"

Susan's authoritative voice, and Farnsworth's apparent readiness to assist her, if she delayed, persuaded Mrs. O'Brien to leave the car. She went into the kitchen with Susan, and Patty turned a beaming face to Bill.

"It's all right now," she said. "Susan will bring her around. But, oh, Billee, how DID you DARE to do such a thing?"

"I'd dare anything to get you what you want. And you said you wanted that particular cook. So I got her."

"But you'll be arrested for kidnapping!"

"Oh, I think not. I'll telephone over to that second-rate gardener, and I fancy I can make it all right."

Then Bill and Patty sauntered round the house to the veranda.

"Where's your cook?" cried Mona.

"In the kitchen, where she belongs," replied Patty. "Do you want her here?"

"No, but how did you get one?"

"Kidnapped her!" declared Patty, and then amid the

laughter of their hearers, they told the whole story.

"I never heard of such a thing!" said Aunt Adelaide, with a disapproving frown.

"But it was that, or no dinner," said Patty, plaintively.

"I think it's great!" said Roger. "And the end is not yet! In an hour, all sorts of police and detectives and weird things like that will come up here and arrest us."

"They'll only take Patty and me," said Farnsworth, "and we can look out for ourselves, can't we, A. B.?"

But Patty only smiled, and ran away to her own room.

CHAPTER XX

GOOD-BYE FOR NOW

It was the day of Farnsworth's departure. In fact, the whole house party was leaving. Roger had already gone, and the Kenerleys and Daisy Dow were to go next day, while Cromer, who had become attached to Spring Beach, had concluded to transfer himself to a hotel and stay the rest of the summer.

"I hate to have you all go," said Mona, dolefully. "Now that I've new servants, and such good ones, I'd like to have you all stay on indefinitely."

"There are others," suggested Jim Kenerley.

"I know, but I don't want others. This crowd has become so chummy and nice it's a pity to break it up. Aren't you sorry to go, Bill?"

"Haven't gone yet!" said Farnsworth, cheerfully.

"But your things are all packed, and you're to go this afternoon," said Mona.

"Well, it's morning now; why borrow trouble? Let's have some fun instead."

"Yes, let's!" and Mona brightened up. "Let's go on a picnic!"

"I hate picnics," said Daisy; "they're no fun. Let's motor over to Lakeville."

"I hate Lakeville," said Patty. "Let's have a dress-up party of some kind."

"We can't get up a fancy dress party in a few hours," objected Adele Keneriey. "Let's have a contest of some sort, - with prizes. Tennis, - or basket ball."

"Oh, it's too warm for those things," said Laurence Cromer. "Let's do something quieter. I'll tell you what, - let's play Human Parcheesi! Just the thing."

"What IS Human Parcheesi?" asked Patty, interested at once.

"Oh, it's a new game," explained Cromer; "in fact, I just made it up this instant."

"How do you play it?" asked Mona.

"I don't quite know myself yet. I haven't finished making it up. Anyway, you have to have more people. Let me see, we have seven here. Can you get some more, Mona? We won't play till after luncheon. It will take the rest of the morning for me to finish making up the game. We'll play on the west lawn. Oh, it's going to be lovely! I want four billion yards of red ribbon and cosy decorations and a lot of things! Skip to the telephone, Mona, and invite enough people to make twenty of us all together. Tell 'em to come at three o'clock, I'll be ready then."

"Bill has to go away about six," said Mona, doubtfully.

"Well, make 'em come at two, then. The game won't take long, once we get started. Now, I'll select four players. Mona will be one, and Daisy Dow, Jim Kenerley and I will be the others."

Mona was already at the telephone, and the other selected players drew around Cromer to learn what they were to do.

"It's going to be the greatest fun ever," he declared. "If we can't get red ribbon, we'll take twine. Guess it'll be better, anyhow. Mona, will you send a slave to the general store to buy a lot of balls of twine?"

"I'll attend to it," said Patty, "Mona's telephoning."

When Patty returned from this errand, the others were all out on the west lawn. Farnsworth and Jim Kenerley were measuring off spaces, and a gardener was driving in pegs.

When the twine arrived, it was stretched on these pegs, until the whole lawn was diagrammed like a parcheesi board. There were the four squares in the corners, representing "Homes," there was a large square in the centre, and the paths were marked into regular rectangles with a "Safety Spot" in every fifth space.

So carefully was the measuring done that at a short distance it looked exactly like a parcheesi board, except the colouring.

"Now," said Cromer, when the ground was ready, "each of you four 'Players' must fix up your corner

'Homes' with a different colour."

So Daisy chose pink, and Mona blue, and Mr. Kenerley yellow, and Laurence Cromer green.

Rugs of appropriate colours were brought from the house for these "Homes," and a few wicker chairs or campstools were placed in them. Then the spirit of emulation was roused, and the "Players" sought for little tables, vases of flowers, or potted palms to decorate their "Homes."

Mrs. Kenerley helped her husband, and Patty assisted Cromer, with their feminine tastes and ideas, and Patty prevailed on the head gardener to cut his choicest flowers to decorate the game.

"You see," Laurence said, "we COULD get this thing up beautifully, with canopies and flags of the four colours, and turkey red strips down these paths and all that. But this will do for a makeshift game."

The central square was prettily arranged with a set of furniture brought from a veranda, a tea table, a stand of flowers, and a flagpole and flag.

Comfortable seats were arranged here for Mrs. Parsons, and any one else who was merely a spectator of the game. Under Cromer's directions, the girls made sixteen caps and sashes of cheesecloth, four of each colour.

The guests whom Mona invited all came, and soon after two o'clock the game began. The four "Players," each decorated with his or her own colour, went to their respective homes, and from there called out the names of those whom they wished for "Counters." Mona called first, and promptly chose Patty.

When Patty came to Mona's "Home" she was given a blue cap and sash, which she immediately donned.

Daisy was next, and she chose Farnsworth, who went forward to receive his pink cap and sash.

After a time each "Player" had chosen four counters, and the caps and sashes were all proudly worn.

"Now we 'Players,'" Cromer directed, "stay here in our 'Homes,' and we send out our 'Counters,' just as if we were playing real parcheesi. Daisy, you throw your dice first."

Daisy threw the dice which had been provided, and she threw a five and a three.

"Put a counter out with the five," said Cromer, "and let him march three squares for the three."

Amid much laughter and fun, Daisy sent Big Bill Farnsworth out first, and ordered him to march three spaces. This Farnsworth did, and stood waiting for his next move.

Then Jim Kenerley threw, but threw only a three and a four, so he had to wait another turn.

The game proved to be great fun. A five thrown allowed another counter started out, and all other throws meant movements of the counters. A counter on a "Safety Spot" was secure against invaders, but on an unprotected square one might be sent back "Home" to start all over again.

Of course the great central square was the goal, and there refreshing lemonade or iced tea awaited the "Counters." Many were the amusing exigencies. Daisy had just triumphantly put out her last counter when two others were returned ignominiously "Home."

Counters chatted affably with other counters who chanced to be on adjoining squares, or gleefully sent them home, as they invaded the same square.

Patty stood comfortably on a "Safety Spot," with Captain Sayre on the next space but one.

"This is a great game," said she. "Isn't Mr. Cromer clever to invent it? Do you know I already see great possibilities in it. I'm going to get up a fine one for a charity or something."

"Yes, do; I'll help you. Make people pay to be 'Counters,' and then have prizes for those who get all the way around."

"Yes, and then have -"

But Captain Sayre had been moved four spaces away, and was out of hearing distance, though he could still smile and wave his hand at Patty on her "Safety Spot."

As the game progressed, one after another reached the Central Square, but as Jim Kenerley got all four of his "Counters" in first he was declared winner.

Then all ran into the Central Square and soon discovered that "Parcheesi" gave them a good appetite for tea and cakes.

Soon after five the Spring Beach guests went home, charmed with the new game, and promising to play it again some day. The "Red Chimneys" party congratulated Cromer heartily on his clever entertainment, and renewed their lamentations that the house party would be so soon only a memory.

"Let's all go over to the Country Club for a farewell dinner and dance," suggested Jim Kenerley.

"All right," agreed Patty, who was always ready for a dance.

"I can't go," said Farnsworth. "I have to take the six-thirty train, - but you others go on."

"Too bad, old fellow," said Kenerley; "wish you could go. But the rest of you will, won't you?"

They all accepted the invitation, and went away to dress.

Patty hung back a moment to say good-bye to Bill, but Daisy forestalled her.

"Oh, Bill," she said, "walk with me as far as the rose garden. I want to say my farewells to you."

Farnsworth couldn't well refuse, so he went off with Daisy, giving Patty a pleading look over his shoulder which she rightly read to mean that he wanted to see her again before he left.

But Daisy prolonged her interview as much as

possible, with the amiable intention of keeping Patty and Bill apart.

At last Bill said, as they stood on the terrace, "You ought to be dressing, Daisy. You'll be late for the club dinner party."

"No hurry," she said, shrugging her shoulders, "I can go over later."

"How?" asked Farnsworth, suddenly interested.

"Oh, Barker will take me over in a runabout."

"But Barker's to take me to the station. You'd better go with the rest, Daisy."

Something in Bill's tone made Daisy acquiesce, so she said, shortly, "Oh, very well," and turned toward the house.

She went to her room, and Farnsworth looked about for Patty. She was nowhere to be seen, and all the first floor rooms were empty save for a servant here and there. Finally Bill said to a parlourmaid, "Please go to Miss Fairfield and ask her if she will come down and see Mr. Farnsworth just a minute."

The maid departed, and a moment later Patty came down. She was all dressed for the dinner, in a soft, shimmering, pale blue chiffon, and she wore Bill's wreath in her hair.

"Apple Blossom," he said, softly, and his voice choked in his throat.

"I've been trying to get you a moment alone all day," he said, "but I couldn't. I believe you evaded me on purpose!"

"Why should I?" and Patty looked a little scared.

"I'll tell you why! Because you knew what I wanted to say to you! Because you KNOW - confound that butler! He's everywhere at once! Patty, come in the drawing-room."

"Jane's in there," said Patty, demurely, and smiling up at Bill from under her long lashes.

"Well, come, - oh, come anywhere, where I can speak to you alone a minute!"

"Just one minute," said Patty, "no more!"

"All right, but where can we go?"

"Here!" said Patty, and leading him through the dining-room, she opened the door of the butler's pantry, a spacious and attractive room of itself.

"James won't be in here to-night," she said, "as we are dining out. But I'll only stay a minute."

"But, Patty, DARLING, I want to tell you, - you know I'm going away, and I won't see you again, - and I MUST tell you, - I must ASK you -"

"Patty - Pat-ty! Bill! Where ARE you both?"

Mona's voice rose high as she called, and it was joined by others calling the same two names.

"They're calling, we must go!" exclaimed Patty.

"Go! Nothing!" cried Big Bill, savagely. He glanced round, - he saw the dumb-waiter, built large and roomy in accordance with all the plans of "Red Chimneys."

In about three seconds he had picked Patty up, and before she knew it, she found herself sitting on the top shelf of that big dumb-waiter, and, moreover, she found herself being lowered, at first slowly, and then rapidly.

She was about to scream when she heard Big Bill whisper softly, but commandingly, "Not a word! Not a sound! I'll pull you up in a few minutes."

She heard the doors above her close. She was in total darkness. She had no desire to scream, but she was consumed with laughter.

Farnsworth had hidden her! Hidden her from Mona and the others, in the dumb-waiter! What a man he was! She had no idea what he intended to do next, but she was not afraid. It was an escapade, and of all things Patty loved an escapade!

After closing the doors, Bill put out the light in the butler's pantry, opened the door, slipped through the dimly lighted dining-room, and came around by a side hall to the group in the main hall.

"Calling me?" he said. "I was just coming to say good-bye to you all. Where's Patty?"

"That's what we want to know," said Mona. "We thought she was with you."

"She isn't," said Bill, truthfully enough.

"Well, where CAN she be? I've looked everywhere! Even in the pantries."

"Hasn't one load already started?"

"Yes, Aunt Adelaide and the Kenerleys have gone."

"Didn't she go with them?"

"Why, she MUST have done so. Well, good-bye, dear old Bill, come and see us again next summer, won't you?"

"I will so!" and Bill shook Mona's hand mightily, as an earnest of his words.

"And I'm sorry to go off and leave you, but you go to the station in a few minutes, don't you?"

"Yes, and Barker will look after me. Run along, Mona, I'll write you in a day or two, and tell you how much I've enjoyed my visit here."

Some further cordial good-byes were said, and then the car started off with Daisy, Mona, and Cromer to the Country Club. Farnsworth flew back to the pantry.

"Hello," he said, as he drew up the dumb-waiter, "you WILL evade me, will you, you little bunch of perversity?"

Patty, who was still laughing at his daring deed, said, "Have they all gone?" "They sure have! You and I are here all alone."

"Oh, Bill!" and Patty's lip quivered a little. "How COULD you do that? What SHALL I do?"

"Now don't get ruffled, little one; my train goes in twenty minutes. You're going to the station to see me off, and then Barker will take you on to the Country Club to join the rest of them. You won't be half an hour late!"

This wasn't a VERY dreadful outlook, so Patty smiled again.

"Why stay in this queer place?" she said. "Why not go out on the veranda?"

"No; there are eleven hundred servants bobbing up everywhere! Here I can have you all to myself long enough to make you answer one question. Apple Blossom, will you marry me?"

"No, sir; thank you," and Patty blushed, but looked straight into Farnsworth's eyes.

"You mean it, don't you?" he said, returning her gaze. "And why not, little girl?"

"Because, Billee, I don't want to marry anybody, - at least, not for years and years. I like you AWFULLY, - and I appreciate all your kindness, and your, - your liking for me -"

"Don't say liking, sweetheart; it's love, - deep, true, BIG love for you, - you little sunbeam. Oh, Patty, CAN'T you?"

"No, Little Billee, I can't, - but, - but I DO like to have

you love me like that!"

"Then I shall WAIT, dear!" and Bill's voice was full of triumphant gladness. "If you like to have me love you, I can hope and believe that some day you'll love me. You ARE too young, dear, you're just a little girl, I know."

"Why, I'm not even 'out,'" said Patty. "I'm to come out next winter, you know."

"Yes, and then you'll have lots of admirers, and they'll flatter you, but they won't spoil you. I know your sweet, simple, generous nature; it can't be spoiled, even by the foolishnesses of society." "Will YOU come to my coming-out party, Bill?"

"I don't know, perhaps so. I may see you before then. And I'll write to you, mayn't I, Apple Blossom?"

"Oh, yes, do! I love to get letters, and I know I'll love yours."

"DO love them, dear, and perhaps, through them, learn to love, - Jiminetty Christmas, Apple Blossom, I've just ten minutes to catch that train! Come on, dear, fly with me, at least to the railroad station!"

They flew, and by speeding the car, Barker just managed to reach the station in time. The ride was a silent one, but Farnsworth held Patty's hand in a close, warm pressure all the way. As they reached the platform, he bent over her and whispered:

"Good-bye, sweetheart, DEAR little Apple Blossom. Some day I shall come back and win you for my own.

Until then, I shall just wait, - and love you."

A light kiss fell on the little hand he had been holding, and then Farnsworth flung himself out of the motor-car, and on to the platform of the already moving train.

"To the Country Club, Barker," said Patty.

Choose from Thousands of 1stWorldLibrary Classics By

Adolphus WilliamWard
Aesop
Agatha Christie
Alexander Aaronsohn
Alexander Kielland
Alexandre Dumas
Alfred Gatty
Alfred Ollivant
Alice Duer Miller
Alice Turner Curtis
Alice Dunbar
Ambrose Bierce
Amelia E. Barr
Andrew Lang
Andrew McFarland Davis
Anna Sewell
Annie Besant
Annie Hamilton Donnell
Annie Payson Call
Anton Chekhov
Arnold Bennett
Arthur Conan Doyle
Arthur Ransome
Atticus
B. M. Bower
Basil King
Bayard Taylor
Ben Macomber
Booth Tarkington
Bram Stoker
C. Collodi
C. E. Orr
C. M. Ingleby
Carolyn Wells
Catherine Parr Traill
Charles A. Eastman
Charles Dickens
Charles Dudley Warner
Charles Farrar Browne
Charles Ives
Charles Kingsley
Charles Lathrop Pack
Charles Whibley
Charles Willing Beale
Charlotte M. Braeme
Charlotte M.Yonge
Clair W. Hayes
Clarence Day Jr.
Clarence E. Mulford

Clemence Housman
Confucius
Cornelis DeWitt Wilcox
Cyril Burleigh
D. H. Lawrence
Daniel Defoe
David Garnett
Don Carlos Janes
Donald Keyhole
Dorothy Kilner
Dougan Clark
E. Nesbit
E.P.Roe
E. Phillips Oppenheim
Edgar Allan Poe
Edgar Rice Burroughs
Edith Wharton
Edward J. O'Biren
John Cournos
Edwin L. Arnold
Eleanor Atkins
Elizabeth Cleghorn
Gaskell
Elizabeth Von Arnim
Ellem Key
Emily Dickinson
Erasmus W. Jones
Ernie Howard Pie
Ethel Turner
Ethel Watts Mumford
Eugenie Foa
Eugene Wood
Evelyn Everett-Green
Everard Cotes
F. J. Cross
Federick Austin Ogg
Ferdinand Ossendowski
Francis Bacon
Francis Darwin
Frances Hodgson Burnett
Frank Gee Patchin
Frank Harris
Frank Jewett Mather
Frank L. Packard
Frederick Trevor Hill
Frederick Winslow Taylor
Friedrich Kerst
Friedrich Nietzsche
Fyodor Dostoyevsky

Gabrielle E. Jackson
Garrett P. Serviss
Gaston Leroux
George Ade
Geroge Bernard Shaw
George Ebers
George Eliot
George MacDonald
George Orwell
George Tucker
George W. Cable
George Wharton James
Gertrude Atherton
Grace E. King
Grant Allen
Guillermo A. Sherwell
Gulielma Zollinger
Gustav Flaubert
H. A. Cody
H. B. Irving
H. G. Wells
H. H. Munro
H. Irving Hancock
H. Rider Haggard
H. W. C. Davis
Hamilton Wright Mabie
Hans Christian Andersen
Harold Avery
Harold McGrath
Harriet Beecher Stowe
Harry Houidini
Helent Hunt Jackson
Helen Nicolay
Hendy David Thoreau
Henrik Ibsen
Henry Adams
Henry Ford
Henry Frost
Henry James
Henry Jones Ford
Henry Seton Merriman
Henry Wadsworth
Longfellow
Henry W Longfellow
Herbert A. Giles
Herbert N. Casson
Herman Hesse
Homer
Honore De Balzac

Horace Walpole	Laurence Housman	Robert Lansing
Horatio Alger, Jr.	Leo Tolstoy	Robert Michael Ballantyne
Howard Pyle	Leonid Andreyev	Robert W. Chambers
Howard R. Garis	Lewis Carroll	Rosa Nouchette Carey
Hugh Lofting	Lilian Bell	Ross Kay
Hugh Walpole	Lloyd Osbourne	Rudyard Kipling
Humphry Ward	Louis Tracy	Samuel B. Allison
Ian Maclaren	Louisa May Alcott	Samuel Hopkins Adams
Israel Abrahams	Lucy Fitch Perkins	Sarah Bernhardt
J.G.Austin	Lucy Maud Montgomery	Selma Lagerlof
J. Henri Fabre	Lydia Miller Middleton	Sherwood Anderson
J. M. Barrie	Lyndon Orr	Sigmund Freud
J. Macdonald Oxley	M. H. Adams	Standish O'Grady
J. S. Knowles	Margaret E. Sangster	Stanley Weyman
J. Storer Clouston	Margaret Vandercook	Stella Benson
Jack London	Maria Edgeworth	Stephen Crane
Jacob Abbott	Maria Thompson Daviess	Stewart Edward White
James Allen	Mariano Azuela	Stijn Streuvels
James Lane Allen	Marion Polk Angellotti	Swami Abhedananda
James Andrews	Mark Overton	Swami Parmananda
James Baldwin	Mark Twain	T. S. Ackland
James DeMille	Mary Austin	The Princess Der Ling
James Joyce	Mary Cole	Thomas A. Janvier
James Oliver Curwood	Mary Rowlandson	Thomas A Kempis
James Oppenheim	Mary Wollstonecraft	Thomas Anderton
James Otis	Shelley	Thomas Bailey Aldrich
Jane Austen	Max Beerbohm	Thomas Bulfinch
Jens Peter Jacobsen	Myra Kelly	Thomas De Quincey
Jerome K. Jerome	Nathaniel Hawthrone	Thomas H. Huxley
John Burroughs	O. F. Walton	Thomas Hardy
John F. Kennedy	Oscar Wilde	Thomas More
John Gay	Owen Johnson	Thornton W. Burgess
John Glasworthy	P.G.Wodehouse	U. S. Grant
John Habberton	Paul and Mable Thorn	Valentine Williams
John Joy Bell	Paul G. Tomlinson	Victor Appleton
John Milton	Paul Severing	Virginia Woolf
John Philip Sousa	Peter B. Kyne	Walter Scott
Jonathan Swift	Plato	Washington Irving
Joseph Carey	R. Derby Holmes	Wilbur Lawton
Joseph Conrad	R. L. Stevenson	Wilkie Collins
Joseph Jacobs	Rabindranath Tagore	Willa Cather
Julian Hawthrone	Rahul Alvares	Willard F. Baker
Julies Vernes	Ralph Waldo Emmerson	William Makepeace
Justin Huntly McCarthy	Rene Descartes	Thackeray
Kakuzo Okakura	Rex E. Beach	William W. Walter
Kenneth Grahame	Richard Harding Davis	Winston Churchill
Kate Langley Bosher	Richard Jefferies	Yei Theodora Ozaki
L. A. Abbot	Robert Barr	Young E. Allison
L. T. Meade	Robert Frost	Zane Grey
L. Frank Baum	Robert Gordon Anderson	
Laura Lee Hope	Robert L. Drake